THE FIFTH CURSE

Teas & Temptations Mysteries
Book Five

CINDY STARK

www.cindystark.com

The Fifth Curse © 2019 C. Nielsen

Cover Design by Kelli Ann Morgan
Inspire Creative Services

License Notes

Welcome to Stonebridge, Massachusetts

Welcome to Stonebridge, a small town in Massachusetts where the label "witch" is just as dangerous now as it was in 1692. From a distance, most would say the folks in Stonebridge are about the friendliest around. But a dark and disturbing history is the backbone that continues to haunt citizens of this quaint town where many have secrets they never intend to reveal.

Visit www.cindystark.com for more titles and release information. Sign up for Cindy's newsletter to ensure you're always hearing the latest happenings.

DISCLAIMER:

All spells in this book are purely fictional and for fun.
Not intended for actual use.

PROLOGUE

Stonebridge, Massachusetts 1689

The air in the musty barn was still thick from the heat of the previous day, but Clarabelle barely paid it any mind as she tugged the cow's udders and squirted milk into the dull silver pail. The sounds of the liquid repeatedly hitting metal lulled her into a sense of tranquility, and her thoughts drifted to the handsome Cal Hooton.

Tall and strong. Blond hair that looked soft enough to make her yearn to touch it. Fiery blue eyes that sent her senses reeling.

Best yet, he liked her.

Clarabelle sensed that every time she found herself near him in town and at church. Whether she caught him staring at her or not, she knew he watched her constantly.

She like that.

A sob from behind her broke her reverie, and she jerked around. Her quick movements brought an unhappy moo from the cow.

Eliza approached with quick footsteps, and Clarabelle stood. Tears streaked her reddened cheeks, and anguish poured from her soul.

Familiar panic struck deep in Clarabelle's heart. "Eliza! What is it?"

Her friend threw her arms around Clarabelle's waist and buried her face against her shoulder as she broke and wept.

Clarabelle held her tight and stroked her long blond hair. "Hush. It's okay. Try to calm yourself so you can tell me what happened."

Eliza cried for several more moments before she regained some semblance of control. "It's Emma. They took her."

Clarabelle's heart lurched into her throat. *"No."*

Emma and Eliza had been married within weeks of each other and had struck up a friendship. Clarabelle had spoken to her only a few times, but she liked the warm and sensitive redhead. "They accused her of witchcraft?"

Eliza nodded as more tears flooded her eyes.

"But she's not even a witch."

Her friend clamped a hand over her mouth to cover a sob.

Stonebridge had gone nine months without an incident. Without any unfounded accusations. Without any horrific deaths.

Clarabelle had begun to believe they might have a chance at a future.

Now this.

"Is she still alive?"

Eliza rapidly blinked her wet lashes. "Yes. We must do something, Clarabelle. *We must.*"

They couldn't though. Not without exposing themselves. Once a person had been cast under that dark shadow, nothing could save them.

"There isn't anything we can do, Eliza."

"A curse. Another curse. Something that's worse than their fear of witches."

Eliza's words stunned her. She had always been the cautious one and the most forgiving out of the four of them. To hear her speak vengeance now only proved how far the town had pushed her. All of them.

"Something that will distract them and give Emma a chance," Eliza continued. "Something that will burn hot enough to make them fear for their lives so that they'll forget about her long enough to save her."

Clarabelle wasn't sure it would help, but she couldn't deny Eliza and her friend the chance. "Something like...scorching summer heat? Make it too hot for anyone to be out in the sun? If it's too hot for man or beast, perchance, they'll wait to carry out their sentence."

Eliza's expression brightened, and she sniffed. "Yes. That may help."

Clarabelle glanced about the dim barn and her unfinished chores. "I will need some time before I can slip away. It's best if we attempt this on our own and not involve Lily or Scarlet. I fear they've been under much scrutiny as of late."

Eliza nodded quickly. "There isn't time to gather anyway. I am confident we can manage this on our own."

Clarabelle agreed. The last few years had forced them to hone their skills, and she was certain she and Eliza had enough power between them.

"Meet me beneath the bridge in an hour. Bring a small amount of blessed water and a tiny cauldron if you can manage."

Eliza nodded repeatedly. "Yes. Yes, I can do that."

She gave Clarabelle a swift hug. "I'll see you soon, sister."

****

Clarabelle's heart pounded like gigantic booms of thunder as she gathered a handful of dried summer grass, twigs, and branches and then made her way down the river's embankment. Rocks and dirt slid beneath her and tumbled into the water.

Eliza was already waiting, huddled beneath the structure. Her tears had dried and been replaced by a look of fierce determination. "Did you sneak away without trouble?"

Clarabelle nodded. "But I can't be gone long."

"Same for me." Eliza slid a tiny iron cauldron from her basket. "I encountered John Henry Parrish on my way here."

She widened her eyes as fear iced her veins. "While carrying the cauldron?"

Eliza released a shaky breath. "I feared he'd know what I had. But he and his wife spoke to me only a minute before wishing me a good day."

Clarabelle closed her eyes for a brief, grateful moment. "Thank the Blessed Mother."

"Yes," Eliza agreed and nodded.

"Let's hasten, then. No need to tempt fate twice in a day."

Clarabelle stooped and arranged the twigs. In the center of them, she made a small bird's nest from the dried grass. She stood long enough to remove the bundle she'd tucked into her bodice and opened it to reveal flint and steel along with several sprigs of mint.

She crouched and struck flint against steel, sending tiny sparks into the dried grass. "It would be nice to have Scarlet around to help with this, though."

Eliza chuckled. "She can be useful."

When a small fire crackled and burned, Eliza set the cauldron on top.

"We only need a little water," Clarabelle directed, and Eliza poured in enough to cover the bottom.

Clarabelle added mint leaves, stirring the air with their unmistakable scent. "These represent the cold which can also bite with a certain fierceness."

Eliza nodded. "Good. I'm glad you thought of that. Fire will be the heat. Both can create havoc depending on the season."

"Yes."

The two sat in silence with only the crackling fire and the sounds of birds in the trees to disturb their peace while they waited for the proper time to commence their spell. Energy intensified as the water and mint began to boil, scenting the air with a crisp, fresh smell.

Clarabelle glanced across the cauldron to Eliza. "Are you ready?"

Eliza gave her an assured nod and held out both hands. "Let's pray this works."

She entwined her fingers with her friend's, and power sizzled between them. They'd come a long way from the girls who'd watched the townsfolk murder their friend.

Clarabelle inhaled a deep breath and focused on the cauldron and its contents. "Cast the name of witch to endanger a soul, and it shall bring a penance to this town. Bring forth the bitter sting of a harsh winter or the burning sting of sun. Pain and suffering will be all around. This curse shall begin upon the full moon and continue henceforth until it no longer blooms. Save our sisters. Hear our plea. From here on out..."

She paused to nod at Eliza, so that they could finish the spell together. Before they could speak the final words, however, a bee circled around them and then dove straight into the pot.

They gazed at each other wide-eyed, and Clarabelle searched for what it could mean. Nothing came to mind.

After a moment, Eliza shrugged. Clarabelle repeated her gesture, and then they finished together. "So mote it be."

They both stood. Clarabelle gathered her skirt and used it to protect her hand as she lifted the cauldron from the fire. "Let's make haste."

Eliza kicked dirt over the small fire, and Clarabelle emptied the cauldron's contents into the river.

They waited long enough to allow the water to cool the heated pot. Then Eliza stowed it in her basket, and Clarabelle tucked the flint and steel back into her bodice.

Eliza wrapped her arms around Clarabelle in a fierce hug. "We should know by tonight if our curse worked."

Clarabelle nodded.

But the fact was, Clarabelle didn't need to wait. The heated pulse thrumming through her veins told her all she needed to know. "Blessed be, dear sister."

"Blessed be, Clarabelle."

Clarabelle waited until Eliza was out of sight before she climbed the embankment and hurried home to finish her chores.

Maybe this time, the townsfolk would learn.

CHAPTER ONE
Current Day

Hazel Hardy glanced over the sparkling crystal containers filled with various spiked and regular iced teas. She smoothed the pristine white linen tablecloth they rested on and gave the pink roses and baby's breath sitting in a nearby vase one last sniff.

Most of the people attending the wedding had already entered Stonebridge's oldest church, and it was time for her to as well. The ceremony would begin in ten minutes.

The sun drew closer to evening, and she hurried from beneath the billowy white tent where caterers would serve food during the reception. Her heels wobbled as she crossed the church lawn toward the large rough-hewn wooden doors that had been propped open for the celebration.

Cooler air, scented by the passing of centuries, greeted her as she entered. Cheerful voices echoed from the chapel, along with bounteous happy emotions.

Today was one of those good days in a person's life. She wished Peter could have abandoned his police chief duties and joined her.

As she entered the chapel, she gave an inward chuckle. Someone had finally tricked her into sitting on a church pew.

That was okay. She was glad to share the soon-to-be-wedded couple's happiness.

Hazel searched for Margaret, Peter's administrative assistant and one of her good friends, who had saved her a spot in the second to the last box of seats in the old church. Hazel opened the gate-like door to enter the enclosure and slipped onto the hard, wooden bench beside Margaret.

Her friend had chosen a champagne silk dress and matching hat with an enormous bow that was bigger than her head. Perfect attire if they'd been attending a royal wedding.

Margaret clutched a small purse with one gloved hand and lifted the other to whisper. "Good. You're here. They're almost ready to start."

Hazel smiled and nodded. "Just needed to make sure everything was perfect outside."

"I'm sure it is."

Hazel studied the guests and waited for the soft, melodic tune on the piano to switch to the Wedding March.

Five minutes passed.

Then ten.

Stress and nerves often slowed down ladies on the brink of marriage, but Hazel knew patience would reward the guests with a beautiful bride.

She'd been thrilled when Fiona Hoffstetter had contacted her. She hadn't known her personally, but Fiona's reputation as the best wedding planner in the area preceded her.

Fiona had told her that, although she no longer lived in town, she'd always loved the old church. Stonebridge was the most beautiful, quaint town she knew, and she and her fiancé had grown up in the area.

Fiona had said she'd heard fantastic things about Hazel's specialty teas and asked her to cater the drinks for her upcoming wedding. Coming from Fiona, a wedding planner herself, that was quite the compliment.

Hazel hadn't thought about branching out into catering, but maybe she should.

A snicker from behind them caught Hazel's attention, and she focused her senses in that direction.

"Can you imagine how much she's freaking out right now?" one woman said. "She's probably searching everywhere for her shoes."

Hazel narrowed her gaze, wondering if she'd misunderstood.

"Who's going to notice missing shoes?" another with a higher-pitched voice said. "Her veil is much more important."

Hazel opened her eyes wide and blinked. They'd stolen or hidden the bride's shoes and veil? She yearned to turn to see who could do such a cruel thing.

Margaret did exactly that. "Hush, Gwen. If you can't be nice, you shouldn't have come."

The pianist pounded out the first dramatic notes in the Wedding March, bringing their conversation to a halt. Hazel stood as the flower girl dressed in soft pink tulle scattered peach-colored rose petals down the aisle.

Hazel used the pretense of watching for the bride to enter the chapel as an excuse to turn toward the doors, giving her a perfect view of the women behind her.

She recognized Margaret's sister, Gwen, a voluptuous platinum blonde wearing a lime green dress with dramatic cleavage. She sat with two other twenty-something women. One with long black curls wore a fiery red dress, black gloves, and fantastic red shoes with three-inch heels. The other paled in comparison with light brown hair, dressed in baby blue, who also wore a hat, though not as elaborate as Margaret's.

In Hazel's mind, she couldn't conjure a good enough reason why Gwen and the other two would choose to play a joke on the bride. A woman's wedding day should be one of the most memorable in her life and already had enough anxiety to last for weeks.

Whispers in the crowd quieted as the veil-less bride stepped through the doors. Her flushed face carried obvious signs of stress, and she narrowed her gaze when she spotted the three women in the back row.

She knew.

As Fiona passed Hazel's pew, she stumbled. A quick snort of laughter escaped the woman in red, and her friends giggled in response. The bride's father placed a firm hand on Fiona's waist to steady her, and Hazel noticed her dress seemed a tad long.

Probably because of the lack of shoes.

Hazel caught sight of the nasty women's faces as they shifted to follow the bride's progress. They were all too focused on Fiona to notice Hazel's perusal. She wondered if Margaret was aware of their underhanded tactics.

Fiona's father kissed her cheek and handed her off to her beloved, a man named Arthur Wainswright.

"Wait until the itching starts," one of the women said, and they all three giggled.

Seconds after the words reached Hazel's ears, poor Fiona pretended to adjust the strap on her dress, but Hazel could see she'd used the action to cover her forearm rubbing across one of her breasts.

Hazel shook her head in complete disgust, wishing she could cast a small hex on the three women so they would know what humiliation felt like.

Hazel suffered empathetically through the entire ceremony, feeling every inch of Fiona's discomfort and anxiety. When the priest announced them as husband and wife and Arthur leaned in for a kiss, Hazel turned, prepared to give the women a piece of her mind.

But they were gone.

Margaret huffed in disgust. "I cannot believe Gwen."

Hazel absorbed some of Margaret's embarrassment. "Sounds like the three of them played some nasty tricks on Fiona. Shoes? Veil? Something itchy?"

Margaret rolled her eyes. "I should have known Gwen wouldn't keep her promise to behave. Granted, she does have a right to be angry, but still."

That piqued her curiosity. "Why is she angry with Fiona?"

Her friend widened her eyes. "You haven't heard? Oh, my goodness. You're probably the only person in Stonebridge who hasn't."

Now, she really had her. "Tell me. You know I love a juicy story."

Margaret cast her gaze about them, but everyone seemed preoccupied on making their way to congratulate the newlyweds. "I shouldn't spread gossip since she's my sister, but if she's going to act this way, no one is going to forget anyway."

Hazel nodded in agreement.

"Fiona planned Gwen's wedding a few months back, before you arrived. Gwen had gained a few pounds between trying on her dress and the day of the wedding. When Gwen put on the dress, and it didn't fit, she panicked. I mean totally freaked out."

"I can only imagine."

"Well, Fiona stepped in to save the day and let out a seam. Gwen opted to not wear a bra to give her even more room."

Hazel sucked in a breath, fearing where this conversation might head.

Margaret must have caught the look on her face because she nodded. "Yep. That's right. They'd taken their vows. Gwen lifted her arms to place them around his neck for the kiss, and *rip....*" She screeched the last word.

As much as Hazel didn't approve of Gwen's behavior today, compassion for the poor woman flooded her. "Oh, no. How horrible."

"The guests got an eyeful, and Gwen ran to the dressing room and wouldn't come out for the whole reception. She believes Fiona should have known the thin threads of the remaining seam wouldn't hold, and she won't forgive her."

Hazel lifted her eyebrows and let them drop. What a mess. "Maybe she will now that she's gotten her revenge?"

Margaret snorted, the sound not matching her demure outfit. "Doubtful."

Her friend stood. "Enough of that. Let's go congratulate the couple."

CHAPTER TWO

During the ceremony, decorators had finished the transformation of the back garden of the church, leaving Hazel to feel as though she'd stepped into a fairytale setting. A huge full moon hovered directly above them. Tiny white lights and pink lanterns floated through the trees and over the tables.

Creamy lace lay atop soft pink tablecloths, and the clusters of tiny pink roses, elegant white roses and baby's breath drew the eye to the centers of the tables and added to the charming look.

Margaret released a dreamy sigh as they neared Hazel's tea station. "This is incredible. I feel like we're in a different world."

From the sounds of others passing by, many agreed. "A wedding planner's wedding *should be* the highlight of the season, I'd think."

Hazel slipped behind the waist-high table, while Margaret stepped up to be her first patron. "Tell me what delicious concoctions you've created for us this time."

She grinned, proud of the latest, spiked iced teas she'd crafted specifically for this event. "Something yummy. I have my new pineberry bush tea or original iced tea with lemon and then a couple of fruit-infused alcohol-spiked iced teas."

Margaret placed the back of her gloved hand on her forehead in a dramatic gesture. "Please, give me something spiked. I'll need it to deal with my sister."

Hazel chuckled. "In that case, I have a sweet tea made from orange pekoe and golden rum, and then another I specifically designed with the couple in mind, a lovely hibiscus tea and blueberry vodka combination."

"Give me the hibiscus and blueberry. Sounds divine."

Hazel added a scoop of ice to one of the tall, thin glasses provided to her and poured the purplish concoction over it.

Margaret took a sip and smiled. "Peter's going to be mad he missed this."

She gave her a disappointed look. "That's what happens when you're the big boss and the town needs you."

"Pfft. The man thinks the operation won't run unless he's there, and he works harder than he needs to." She pointed a finger at Hazel. "You should work on fixing that."

A bubble of happiness burst inside her. She liked knowing that he was hers to fix. Whether she could or not was another matter, but he was hers. "I'll get right on that."

Margaret held up her glass in a mock toast, and the D.J. opened with an upbeat, love song that filled the air with a lively energy. "Here's to family. Wish me luck," she said over the music.

Hazel smiled as Margaret walked away. From day one, she'd liked Margaret and understood why Peter did, too, even though she sassed him. She was a good lady.

As someone approached, Hazel shifted her gaze in that direction. Her smile dropped to a dull frown.

Victor strode toward her, looking every inch the sexy, bad boy, dressed to the nines in an Armani suit, his smile bright enough to heat the northern hemisphere.

"Hello, goddess." He sidled up next to her and traced her with a slow, lazy gaze, from bare shoulders to the tips of her pink-polished toes, an action that used to set her on fire. "What do they call that color you're wearing? Fuchsia?"

She'd fallen in love with the flirty dress when she'd lived in Boston. But now she wished she hadn't worn it.

She kept her tone monotonous. "Yes, Victor. It's fuchsia."

He tilted his head to the side and glanced over her again. "It does amazing things for your—"

"Thank you, Victor. But I didn't wear this dress for you, so stop looking."

He glanced across the crowd of guests. "I don't see that drip you're dating in the vicinity. You look lonely."

Someone give her patience. "Peter is at work, and I'm quite fine, Victor. Not lonely at all. When did you say you were headed back to Boston?"

He lifted a corner of his mouth into a sexy grin. "Not yet. I find that I'm enjoying this quaint town. The people are genuine, if not enlightened."

She couldn't disagree with that. "Perhaps you'd like a drink, and then you can go mingle with all your new friends."

His gaze drifted to her cleavage and then back to her face. "Perhaps I would. What do you have?"

"You don't seem like the hibiscus-blueberry type of person, so you can have the orange rum one."

He seemed agreeable to that, so she poured him a glass. He sipped and nodded, and a couple stepped up behind him.

Hazel pointed to them. "I have others I need to take care of."

He glanced over the crowd. "Same. Catch you later." He sauntered off as if he owned the world.

Her employee, Gretta, would arrive to help serve the guests after she closed the teashop for the evening. In the meantime, her younger, blonder sister, Katie had offered to man the station with Hazel, and she was grateful for the extra pair of hands.

An hour later, the party was in full swing, and Gretta had joined them as well to help serve the guests. Many had indulged in several glasses of spiked ice tea or the champagne also offered, leaving the evening atmosphere full of high energy.

The waxing gibbous moon's presence increased the intensity.

From Hazel's point of view, it appeared the bride had left behind the residual stress from the ceremony, laughing and dancing with her husband on their magical night.

Hazel shifted her gaze across the crowd and found the three bridezillas sulking at a table near the dance floor. They shot visual daggers at Fiona who didn't seem to notice. Margaret was nowhere to be found.

Hazel turned to Gretta and Katie. "I'm going to take a break and visit with some friends."

Gretta, looking smart in a tuxedo-inspired outfit assured her with a nod and shooed her away. "Got this covered, boss. Go have some fun."

Hazel paused to load a tray with four spiked iced teas and made her way to the bridezilla table. "You all look like you could use a drink."

Gwen gave her a half-smile as she accepted a glass of the orange-rum tea. "You're Margaret's friend, right?"

"That's right. I'm Hazel. I know your name is Gwen, but I haven't had the pleasure of meeting your friends."

Gwen pointed toward the slender one with light brown hair. Her features were plain, but she had a pleasant spirit. "I'd like you to meet, Carol."

Then she turned her finger toward the one with the stunning red dress and a sassy spirit to match. "And Sondra."

Hazel met their gazes with a friendly smile. She slid into a vacant chair and took the remaining glass of tea.

Sondra lifted her glass. "These are amazing. Margaret said you make them from scratch."

She nodded. "I handcraft all my teas. You should stop into my shop sometime."

"Maybe next time we visit," Carol said. "We're from Salem and don't plan on spending the night."

"Salem," Hazel said with a nod. "You must be friends of Fiona's?"

All three of them snorted or groaned in disagreement at Hazel's trigger question. Sondra wagged a finger at Hazel. "Don't ever call that piece of trash my friend."

Hazel raised surprised, but not necessarily shocked, brows. "That seems a bit harsh, especially considering you're at her wedding."

Carol drained her glass and set it on the table hard enough to be heard over the DJ's voice as he announced the next song. "Considering she swindled me out of the down payment on my house, I don't think that's harsh at all."

This time Hazel was shocked. "She did?"

Carol nodded.

Sondra pointed toward the dancing couple. "Do you see that groom over there?"

It was hard to miss him. "Yes."

"Three months ago, *we* were engaged to be married, and Fiona was helping to plan *our* wedding." Her voice hitched. "At least until she slept with my fiancé."

Gwen sent her a consoling look. "If that's the kind of man he is, you wouldn't want him anyway."

"That's right," Carol added. "He'll probably cheat on her, too. And when she's wallowing in her tears, she'll know that's the same pain she caused you."

Sondra sniffed. "I'd rather have her cheat on him so he knows how it feels to be betrayed."

Funny how Hazel had a completely different opinion of the three women than from earlier in the day. "Be patient. Karma will get them. Always does."

Sondra wiped tears from her eyes and nodded.

Gwen gave her a dry look. "I'm sure you've already heard about my fiasco."

Hazel wanted to deny it to allow the woman to save face but couldn't lie. Instead, she sent her a commiserating look and nodded.

"See?" Gwen said, throwing her hands up in the air. "I will never live that down."

Sondra half-laughed and half-cried. "At least you have a nice set of knockers to show off."

Carol agreed with a nod. "And you're not broke and still living with your new husband at your controlling mother's house."

Hazel could imagine that one all too well. "Ouch. Not the best for a newlywed couple."

Carol snorted. "No. I just pray he won't divorce me before we can save up enough money to get out of there. Fiona took every dime we'd saved for our house."

Sondra stood and wiped at the watery black streaks trailing down her cheeks. "I need to check my face."

She strode across the grass with slumped shoulders and pain radiating from her aura. But her friends were right. She was better off without him.

Fiona was starting to sound more and more like a selfish, cruel person. That or a complete idiot with no morals.

Hazel leaned in. "I have to tell you. I overheard you during the ceremony talking about her veil and shoes. You took them? And itching powder?"

The two women shared a glance, and then Carol met her gaze. "I'm not saying we did or didn't, but if we managed to make her day as miserable as she made ours, she deserved it."

Gwen flicked a finger toward Fiona and her stolen groom. "Problem is she doesn't look miserable."

Hazel wanted to give them all a big hug. "That's why it's best to let Karma handle matters. You all need to focus on healing yourselves and moving forward."

Carol shook her head. "Even if she's over it now, I still say it was worth it."

Gwen snickered. "Did you see how many times she tried to sneak a scratch on her boobs?"

They shared a laugh. So much for them listening to her advice. Still, Hazel knew if they supported each other that way, they'd be okay in the end.

Her tablemate's gazes all flew to just beyond her shoulder, and she sensed Victor before he said a word.

"Hey, goddess. How about a dance?"

"Goddess?" Gwen murmured with longing in her voice. "I want someone to call *me* goddess."

Hazel gritted her teeth and turned toward him. "No, thank you."

The bridezillas gaped at her like she was crazy.

"Come on. It's just a dance."

"No."

He grinned. "I guess I could sit with you instead and fill these lovely ladies in on the details about our sordid past."

"Oooh?" Gwen sounded intrigued. Carol watched them with an interested gaze.

"We have no sordid past, Victor. Go away."

He placed a warm hand on her bare shoulder, and it was all she could do to not cause a scene. "What about the time we—"

"Fine." She stood abruptly. "One dance, and then you leave."

Pure male satisfaction poured from him, and she wanted to punch him in the nose. "One dance. For now." He winked at the ladies as they walked away.

Hazel wanted to tell Gwen she'd gladly flash a crowd if it meant she'd never have to see Victor again. She didn't know if she could actually go through with it, but it was worth considering.

He led her to the dancing area and wrapped a firm hand around her waist. Stirrings of their past love flitted through her, and she squashed them. She reminded herself she'd been in love with the idea of him, the outside as she'd explained to Cora. Not the rotten inside.

A bee whizzed past her, catching her attention not only because she rarely saw them flying during the evening hours, but also because of the speed it jetted through the crowd.

Someone yelped, and she drew her brows together in shock. She couldn't see who'd cried out, but she'd swear that bee had been on a mission and had succeeded.

Very odd.

Victor gave her a wistful smile as their bodies moved together. "You really are a beautiful woman, Hazel."

"And you are a cad, Victor."

He grinned. "I like it when the fire in you stirs."

She rolled her eyes. "I'm more in tune with the earth. Not fire."

"You can't lie to me, Hazel." He twirled her before their bodies met again. "I've seen your fire."

The best man spoke loudly into the microphone, cutting the dance short. "Ladies and gentlemen. Can I have your attention? I'd like to make a toast to the happy couple."

Hazel slipped from Victor's arms. "Looks like I'm needed. Bye." She strode toward the tea station and didn't look back.

The guests quieted down as they lifted their glasses. The groom joined the best man where he stood next to the DJ. Both men glanced across the crowd.

The best man lifted the microphone to his lips as Hazel stepped in beside Gretta. "Fiona? Where are you?"

His words screeched through the speakers, and Hazel and Gretta both grimaced.

Gretta bumped her elbow and leaned close. "Someone needs to take that away from him before he shatters our eardrums."

Hazel agreed with a nod. "He's indulged in one too many drinks and probably has no clue how loud he is."

They both chuckled.

The groom took control of the microphone. "Fiona, love?" He glanced over the crowd. "Has anyone seen my wife?"

Fiona's mother, seated at a table near the front, raised her hand. "She went to the ladies' room a bit ago. Let me check on her."

The funny, somewhat round lady that Hazel had met earlier waddled toward the church's open doors.

"Bad timing," Gretta whispered.

Hazel nodded and hoped the three bridezillas hadn't somehow slipped Fiona laxatives, too.

Several moments passed while the crowd waited. Then a piercing scream ripped through the soft evening air, sending everyone into a panic. The groom shoved off from the best man and ran toward the church.

Hazel should have stayed where she was and minded her own business but couldn't. "I'm going to see."

Gretta gripped her elbow and followed. "Me, too."

Before they and several others reached the door, the groom reappeared, his face paler than moonlight mist, his features etched with shock.

"Call for help! Fiona's dead!"

CHAPTER THREE

Hazel and Gretta made their way inside while they waited for the summoned emergency services to arrive. She'd wanted to see Peter this evening, to show off her fun dress, but not this way.

They followed the sounds of distress and found Mrs. Hofstetter crumpled on the floor and wailing next to her lifeless daughter. She gripped her with a possessive hand and bawled into her silk dress.

The bride's new husband sat on the other side, holding her hand and stroking her cheek. Rivers of grief rolled down his face as he stared at the woman who'd been his bride for mere hours. He shook his head repeatedly but didn't mutter a word or look up at them.

Incredible sadness enveloped Hazel like a cloak, making her feel as though she, too, might die, and she took a step back.

The sound of sirens screaming through the night brought her little relief. The pain from this death would go on for a long, long time for these poor people.

Mrs. Hofstetter shifted, and Hazel's gaze zeroed in on the vivid red and purple marks on Fiona's neck. She gasped and quickly put a hand to her mouth to cover it. Gretta shot her a concerned look.

Hazel slid her thumb and fingers around her own throat and then stuck out her tongue as though choking. Gretta glanced toward Fiona's body. When her eyes widened, Hazel knew she'd noticed the same.

Gretta gave her a soft nudge and discreetly pointed toward the crumpled veil that lay not far from Fiona.

Hazel lifted her brows in a silent question, asking if that's what might have strangled Fiona. Gretta gave a small shrug.

Commotion in the halls signaled that the authorities were on the scene. Several of Peter's officers entered the room, bringing a rush of energy, and scanned it for a quick assessment. Peter walked in right behind them.

Hazel hurried to his side and leaned close to his ear to whisper. "I believe she's been murdered. You might want to have your men keep anyone from leaving."

He agreed with a jerk of his head. "Kennington, gather the guests from outside and put them in the chapel. Try to keep them calm, but let them know they may be here a while."

Peter gave her hand a quick squeeze. "That includes you and Gretta. You'll have to wait in the chapel. After we get the scene secure, I'll interview you along with everyone else and get more details."

She wanted to complain that she wasn't everyone else, but she knew he'd follow protocol and get to her when he could. She also hated that she always had to bow out right in the middle of the action.

Still, there was no point in arguing. "Come on, Gretta. I want to sit somewhere in the back where I can watch everyone."

Fifteen minutes later, Hazel studied the crowd gathered in the chapel. Some whispered. Others outright spread the gossip.

Fiona was dead. Strangled by her veil.

Hazel tried to remember who else had been in the room where Fiona had died so she could pinpoint the source of the rumors. Technically, she knew the information was likely correct. But people should have the decency to respect those who'd lost their loved one that night.

She sighed. Then again, it was hard to control human nature. Including hers.

Gretta lifted her head from her palm to survey Hazel. "Everything okay?"

"Yeah. It's just awful." She narrowed her gaze and glanced around. "Hey, where is your sister?"

"She left maybe ten minutes after you went to visit with your friends."

Hazel raised her brows, and Gretta chuckled. "Take off your investigator's hat. Katie didn't even know Fiona. Also, I remember Fiona was dancing with her father when Katie left, because she mentioned her dad was also short."

Hazel released a chuckle to hide her embarrassment. "Sorry."

Gretta winked. "That's all right. You forgave me for dousing you with holy water. I think I can overlook you considering my sister a murder suspect."

She chuckled. "I think Peter is rubbing off on me."

Gretta shifted in her seat, her vibes anxious and antsy. "I wish they'd let us bring in the teas and some of the goodies. We might be here all night."

"I hope we're not."

Hazel studied the room again and found Margaret sitting with her sister and Sondra. She searched the perimeter around them, but couldn't see Carol. She stood. "Excuse me for just a minute. I'm going to see how Margaret is doing."

Gretta nodded and pulled out her phone. "I'll distract myself with social media. Heaven knows, that can suck up hours without me noticing."

Hazel agreed and then made her way to Margaret. "Hey, guys. Doing okay?"

Gwen's pallor looked ashen, while Sondra appeared downright scared.

"Not so much," Margaret answered. "They're worried our cops will discover their antics." She shot them both with a sharp gaze. "As well they should be."

Gwen looked close to tears. "You promised you wouldn't tell," she said to Margaret.

Margaret dropped her face into her palm. "I said I wouldn't volunteer the information, but if I'm questioned, I'm not going to lie to cover your butt."

Hazel glanced about them again. "Where's Carol?"

All three of their gazes turned guilty. Margaret blew out a breath heavily-laced with anxiety. "She said she needed to use the restroom about ten minutes ago. She managed to get out before Peter posted a man at the door."

Oh, dear. "It shouldn't have taken her that long."

Margaret shook her head, and worry etched her face. "No."

Gwen lifted her gaze and met Hazel's. "She went to find Fiona's shoes that she'd hidden," she whispered. "She needed to wipe off her prints."

"What?" Margaret's voice exploded through the chapel.

Hazel took Margaret's hand and shook her head. "Keep calm."

Margaret pinned her sister with a harsh look. "You didn't tell me that."

Gwen responded with an angry whisper. "Because you would have freaked out, which is exactly what you're doing."

"Of course, I freaked out. Do you realize what this means?"

Sondra glanced at them with a hollow gaze. "She could have killed Fiona."

Gwen gasped. "No."

Sondra snorted, looking like she now wanted to cry, too. "We don't know that. She was really angry."

Gwen folded her arms. "I don't believe that."

Hazel turned to Margaret. "We need to find her. Any idea where she might be?"

"The kitchen," Sondra answered in a despondent voice.

"I'm coming," Gwen announced.

Margaret gave her a snide look. "No, you'll stay right here and try not to look as guilty as you do now. Besides, Officer Bartles might let Hazel and me leave the chapel, but he's not going to let you, especially not without casting suspicion on yourself."

Gwen and Sondra sat like granite lumps of despair as Hazel walked away with Margaret in tow.

However, when they approached John Bartles at the entrance to the chapel, Margaret took the lead. "Hey, John. We need to find Peter. Do you know where he's at?"

"Probably still with the body, I'd guess."

"Thanks." Margaret stepped past him and into the hall.

When Hazel tried to do the same, John grabbed her arm, sending a jolt of fright through her. She tried to fight back her nerves as she met his gaze.

"Just wanted to say I'm sorry, Hazel, for the way I handled your questioning in Father Christopher's case. I was out of line and never should have doubted you."

Relief rushed through her, and a warm smile curved her lips. Part of her really did like the guy. "It's okay. You were just doing your job."

He gave her a grateful nod. "Thanks for understanding."

She returned the gesture and slipped past him. When they were halfway down the deserted hallway, she emptied her lungs. "I thought he was going to stop me."

Margaret snorted. "He's still walking on thin ice with the boss. He wouldn't dare."

Instead of heading toward the main part of the crime scene, Hazel and Margaret turned toward the kitchen.

The room was dim, lit only by a small light burning over the stove. Shadows hid whatever lurked in the corners. Hazel couldn't see Carol, but she could sense her.

"Carol," she whispered. "It's Hazel and Margaret. Where are you?"

Margaret shook her head. "I don't think she's in here."

Hazel nodded. "Carol? Come out, and let us help you. We know why you're here and what you're doing."

Slowly, one of the shadows to the left of Hazel grew larger. Margaret sighed in relief and strode toward her. "Thank heavens."

Or the Blessed Mother, Hazel thought.

Margaret reached her and put a hand on her shoulder. "What do you think you're doing?"

Carol sucked in an emotional breath. "I need to find the shoes. I hid them in a cupboard. The one with the pans, I'm sure. But they're not there."

Margaret clucked. "I can't believe the mess you three have created. I know you're upset. Maybe you're mistaken about which cupboard."

Hazel wanted to warn Margaret not to get too involved in a murder investigation. For all they knew, she might be helping the killer. But she couldn't bring herself to say it, so she observed and took mental notes instead.

Carol sniffed and dragged a forefinger beneath her nose. "I've checked all of them. Twice. But now the cops are everywhere, and I'm afraid to do anything."

Margaret shook her head. "It's best if you head back to the chapel and try to avoid looking suspicious."

"They'll find the shoes," she cried.

"They may, but at this point, staying here will only make you look guiltier. My best advice is to own what you've done. Tell the police outright before they discover evidence that will make you look guilty."

Carol shook her head. "I can't. If my husband finds out...if my mother finds out, they'll kill me."

Margaret straightened and put her hands on her hips. "Would you rather have them mad or find yourself in jail?"

Hazel could tell by her tone that she'd lost her patience.

Margaret gripped Carol's elbow. "Let's go."

The three of them turned toward the exit, but made it no more than a couple of steps when a bright light shone in their faces, blinding them.

"Hold it right there."

CHAPTER FOUR

Hazel hung her head as one of Peter's officers marched her, Margaret and Carol down the hall toward the murder scene. When they arrived, he called Peter out to join them.

Peter narrowed his gaze and folded his arms across his broad chest as he surveyed the three of them. Normally, Hazel loved staring into his devastating green eyes and imagining running her fingers through his dark wavy hair, but, this time, she had a hard time holding his gaze.

"Found these three skulking around the kitchen," Officer Larsen announced.

Margaret inhaled a sharp breath. "We weren't skulking."

Peter gave a slow nod. "Thanks, Larsen."

Then he pointed to Carol. "Why don't you escort this one to the classroom where we'll start interrogations? I'll talk to the others in a separate room."

Larsen nodded and led Carol down the hall.

Peter shook his head in disappointment at Hazel and Margaret. "You two, follow me."

His long strides and stiff posture warned Hazel of his mood, and she silently cursed the bad decisions she'd made that led her to this point.

Peter opened the door to the now-vacant secretary's office and let them precede him. Once inside, he closed the door with a thud of finality, reminding Hazel of a cell door locking her in.

He closed his eyes and exhaled a deep breath before he met their gazes again. "Could one of you give me a reasonable excuse as to why my girlfriend and my administrative assistant blatantly ignored my orders?"

Hazel bit her bottom lip and sensed Margaret's energy shrink beside her. Hazel tried to find the right words, but none would come. Margaret didn't speak either, and Hazel could only guess it was for the same reason.

"Well?" he demanded. "It's one thing for Hazel to ignore me, but you, Margaret, your job depends on how well you follow my instructions."

She threw her hands up in defeat. "I'm sorry, Peter. It's complicated."

He made a show of glancing at his watch. "It appears I'll be here all night anyway, so spill."

Hazel hated experiencing friction between two of the people she loved most. "We were only trying to help Carol."

He shifted a disappointed gaze toward her. "And how exactly did you plan to do that in a darkened kitchen?"

She couldn't see any way out of the corner he'd backed them into. Margaret had made a promise to her sister, but Hazel hadn't. She'd take one for the team this time. "Carol was looking for the shoes she'd hidden earlier."

He shot her an impatient look. "And?"

She exhaled. Here goes nothing. "The short version of a long story is that there are three women who came to the wedding to make Fiona pay for the misery she'd caused them."

Margaret winced and shook her head.

Hazel hadn't meant to cast them all as prime suspects. "Okay, that's worse than it sounded. In the not so distant past, Fiona wrecked their weddings in one way or another, and the three wanted to get even. By playing practical jokes," she hurried to add.

Peter leaned against the desk and folded his arms. "Go on."

"One of them, Gwen, is Margaret's sister and obviously not a killer."

He pulled out the trusty notepad from his shirt pocket, and she sensed Margaret's anxiety heighten, which, in turn, increased hers as well. "There's Gwen, Carol and Sondra. Between them, they stole the bride's shoes and veil and hid them from her, and someone doused the bride's dress with itching powder."

Margaret rolled her eyes and shook her head. "Just the bodice," she corrected. "To make up for Gwen's...exposure."

A hint of a smile appeared on Peter's lips as he jotted in his notebook. "I do recall that incident."

He glanced up at them. "How does this lead us to the kitchen?"

Margaret nervously tugged on the ends of her gloves. "After we'd heard Fiona had been murdered by the veil Sondra had hidden, no less, Carol panicked. Her prints were on the shoes, and she didn't want to be tied to a murder she didn't commit."

"So, the shoes she was looking for were Fiona's?"

"Yes," Hazel answered.

Peter tilted his head and studied her. "Are you sure she didn't do it?"

Margaret scoffed. "Of course, she didn't. None of them did. They might have been angry, but not enough to commit murder."

Hazel cursed herself for not being able to keep her mouth closed. "Except Sondra, maybe. She still carries a lot of anger. Well, Carol kind of, too."

All of them really.

Margaret shot her a look that branded her as a traitor. "I'm sorry, but I don't agree. After Gwen befriended these women because of similar circumstances, I've gotten to know them, too. They all seem like decent people."

Peter studied his assistant. "Can you vouch for their whereabouts all evening?"

She pursed her lips together, not happy with his question, and then shook her head.

"Then they'll remain on the suspect list until proven otherwise."

He released a heavy sigh. "I have to say, I'm really disappointed in you both that you couldn't trust me with this."

A gasp exploded from Margaret. "Excuse me, but I *was* trying to convince Carol to confess what she knew to the police seconds before Larsen found us in the kitchen."

His demeanor lightened. "And did she agree?"

Margaret stared at him.

"No," Hazel said in a low voice. "She was too scared."

Peter straightened. "As she should be."

He walked to the door and then paused. "I'm going to send Larsen in here with some paper. I want you both to write out your recollection of the day. *Every detail.* Then I'm going to have him take you home since I'll no longer require your *assistance* in my investigation."

He left the room and closed the door firmly behind him.

Margaret walked to a chair and dropped into it. Hazel could tell she and her soul were weary, as was Hazel's.

Hazel sought out the chair on the opposite side of the desk, remembering all too well when she'd broken into the files in this very office. With Victor's help, unfortunately.

The worry lines on Margaret's forehead increased. "That didn't go well."

"Nope."

"I hope he won't fire me."

Hazel sent her a kind smile. "He won't. He relies on you so much that he'd completely flounder without you."

Margaret agreed with a small nod of her head. "I hope so."

Hazel drew her brows together. "I hope he doesn't break up with me."

A smile teased Margaret's lips. "Are you kidding? That man is so smitten with you."

Hazel breathed easier, recognizing the truth in Margaret's words. If he hadn't dumped her for being a witch, then he could surely handle a little meddling in his investigation. It wasn't as if she hadn't helped him before.

Though this time, she hadn't offered help. Only hindrance.

CHAPTER FIVE

Hazel had been summoned. That was the only way she could describe Peter's short phone call and their abrupt conversation.

She opted to ride her bike to Peter's house, which gave her time to compose her thoughts and search for a decent excuse for her behavior.

Maybe she should claim peer pressure.

Or friendship.

None really seemed to work. When it came right down to it, she was as guilty as Margaret for interfering, even though she'd only observed what had happened when they'd gone searching for Carol and the missing shoes.

She coasted into the driveway of a gray nineteenth century home with gorgeous decorative trim, her tires bumping over the uneven cement surface. She parked her bike next to his truck in the drive and tried not to drag her feet to the front door.

Red and yellow mini roses were in full bloom along the house, interspersed with lavender and white daisies. Tall pines flanked the corners, sentries planted to protect the house and its occupants, a sure sign that, at some point, a witch had once lived there.

Buzzing sounds hovered nearby, but she couldn't spot the perpetrators. Still, they left her nervous.

She knocked loudly on the door and hoped he'd answer soon.

The moment he opened the door, she forced her way inside and insisted he shut it immediately. "I think you must have a hornet's nest or beehive nearby. Lots of buzzing going on out there."

He responded to her statement with a somber look. "I've heard them, too."

The seriousness of his mood forced her to school her features into the same. She studied his gaze and the energy he emitted to assess his mood. Not the happiest person, but no longer angry.

He turned toward the living room without pulling her into his arms as he usually did.

She frowned.

His house smelled slightly of coffee, which wasn't surprising for a Sunday morning. He didn't have much clutter, but the throw pillows for the couch lay tossed aside on the floor, and a stack of unopened newspapers rested on the coffee table next to a mug.

She caught up to him and placed her hand on his arm. "I'm so sorry, Peter. When I tried to help Margaret find Carol, I had no intention of messing with your investigation."

He turned, his eyes sharply focused on her. "Umm-hmm."

It bothered her that he didn't seem to believe her. And worse, that he hadn't kissed her yet.

She circled in front of him, slid her arms around his waist, and pressed her cheek to his chest. "I know you're mad at me, and you probably don't want a hug, but I've missed you."

She would have died if he didn't hug her back, but he did, and she relaxed in his arms, tilting her face upward to see him. She dropped a quick glance at his lips, hinting at what she wanted, and then met his gaze again.

He narrowed his eyes. "I can't kiss you and stay mad."

She allowed a tiny smile to curve her lips. "Then don't stay mad. You'll eventually forgive me. I can't bear to think what would happen if you didn't. So, you might as well do it now and give me what we both want."

He shook his head slowly but lowered his mouth to hers.

Sparks erupted like firecrackers inside her, and she pressed harder against him, needing to soak up as much of his energy as possible.

She really had missed him in the two days since the murder. He'd barely texted with her, stating he was too busy.

He pulled back and studied her eyes.

She placed a hand over his cheek. "I feel really off when I don't see you. Like a piece of me is missing." Or like someone had punched a hole in their tapestry.

"I feel disturbingly the same."

She lifted questioning brows. "Disturbingly?"

He snorted and pulled from her. "Like you've taken part of my life force, so when you're not around, I don't function the same, as crazy as that sounds."

She smiled. "I think it sounds wonderful, except when we're apart. Will you forgive me?"

He pulled her back into his arms and kissed her hard enough to make her head spin.

Yes, this was exactly what she needed to put her world back on its axis.

"I forgave you days ago, but I don't understand why you couldn't trust me and tell me before you went gallivanting around my crime scene, messing with potential suspects."

She schooled her features into contrition. "Margaret was trying to protect her sister and by extension her sister's friends, who she believed to be innocent. I was just trying to help her."

He shook his head. "I wish you two could learn when to help and when to let things be."

She gave a sheepish shrug. "We'll work on it."

She turned from him and glanced around. "You've never invited me to your house before. I like it. Your home has a nice feel, good vibes."

Hazel met his gaze again. "That only happens when love has left its mark."

She had to admit she envied the relationship he must have had with his wife. She knew Peter liked her a lot, but he'd married Sarah, had pledged his life to her.

She wanted the same.

"Yeah," he glanced toward the pictures on the mantle. "We had some good times."

She gestured with her head toward the fireplace. "Are those pictures of Sarah? Can I look?"

He stared at her for a long moment as though he wasn't certain of his answer and then nodded.

Hazel left his embrace and walked toward the picture of the woman who'd originally stolen Peter's heart. Part of her was jealous that he still had photos of Sarah displayed, but she'd had been an important part of his life, and Hazel needed to honor that.

A woman with auburn hair like hers smiled back from behind the glass in the frame. Pure light radiated from her expression. She'd been happy when that photo had been taken.

"She's beautiful," Hazel said in a reverent voice, feeling him drawing closer behind her.

"Yeah," he said softly. "Inside and out. Not strong like you, but her heart was pure like yours."

She smiled as tenderness welled inside her. It was hard to sort feelings of his loss from her gratitude, so she didn't try.

Peter cleared his throat, and echoes of his agitation filled the room. "I still have a hard time believing she was a witch and never told me. It seems like such a betrayal to our marriage, and I don't want to believe she would do that to us."

Hazel turned and looked up into the devastating green eyes that owned her soul. "Maybe she didn't know."

He nodded thoughtfully. "Like someone might have denied her heritage long ago and not told her children, so that knowledge didn't get passed down?"

"Exactly. Even today, it can be dangerous to show you're a witch. People don't understand the practice, the heritage. Especially in Stonebridge."

He seemed to accept her suggestion, and his angst quieted. "I looked for her hat the other day after we talked about it. I can show you if you'd like."

Oh, definitely. A witch could tell a lot about another from the essence burned into her hat. "I'd love to see it."

He led her through the house and into a back bedroom. The furnishings obviously carried a woman's touch, and Hazel was sure he'd left things as they were before Sarah had died.

A large cardboard box rested on a wooden desk. Peter strode to it and lifted the lid.

Hazel peered inside, almost taken aback by the amount of energy it emitted. She couldn't tell Peter and break his heart, but this woman definitely knew she was a witch. Traces of magic, perhaps even blood magic, filled the space.

She glanced up at Peter. "May I?"

He nodded.

She lifted the black silk hat gently from the box. The brim was trimmed with gold edging and flowered ribbon circled the bottom of the cone. Greenery perched to one side with a gorgeous fiery rose nestled in the center.

She turned it in her hand, loving the detail. She wouldn't insult Peter or Sarah's memory by asking to try it on. "It's very lovely. She made this in a crafting class?"

"Yeah. Several ladies in town would get together once a month for crafting night."

Or a coven meeting.

"Belinda and a couple of others..." His voice trailed off, and he focused on Hazel. "They weren't crafting nights, were they?"

Waves of his pain crashed into her, and she accepted them, hoping to ease his suffering. "I'm not sure. They could have been."

He gave a derisive snort. "Funny how you think you know a person so well."

At that moment, she was terribly grateful she'd come clean about her heritage so that she wouldn't ever cause him similar pain.

She slowly lowered the hat into the box and carefully replaced the lid. Some things were better left alone.

She took his hand and sent him a cheerful smile, hoping it would help. "Hey, I've been here almost twenty minutes, and you haven't told me one thing about the case."

His demeanor turned from hurt to feisty. "And I'm not going to."

Hazel gave Peter a dramatic roll of her eyes and led him back into the living room. "You know you're going to spill the details because you want my help."

He waited a long moment, and she was sure he'd done it to make her suffer.

Then he sighed. "Fine. But only because I struggle to understand women and their emotions when it comes to love and betrayal."

"Like Sondra?" she suggested.

"Exactly. I've tried to question her multiple occasions, but she ends up crying every time, and I have to stop the interview. I don't want to arrest her in order to force information from her, but it might be my only alternative."

"I could try talking to her. She has an antique store in Salem. Margaret could tell me the name." She might even be interested in accompanying her.

He shook his head and snorted. "I can't believe I'm asking you to do this."

She grinned. "Just admit we both know I can be a tremendous asset to you."

He chuckled. "In more ways than one."

His declaration felt like winning the lottery.

"Just don't call Margaret at work," he said. "You'll have to get in touch with her at home."

Curiosity nipped her. "Because you don't want it getting around that I'm acquiring information so I can visit with a murder suspect?"

He met her gaze directly. "No, because I placed her on administrative leave for the time being."

Her emotions dropped to the floor. "You didn't."

He held up a hand. "Don't go getting all upset. Margaret asked if she could. She said it would be hard for her to watch us investigate her sister, and she couldn't promise to be unbiased. I agreed. She's on paid leave, so don't you worry."

She relaxed then and smiled. "You're a good man, Peter Parrish."

His expression seemed to doubt her. "That's what Margaret said, too."

CHAPTER SIX

After Hazel finished her tea deliveries for the morning, she parked her car outside Cora's Café. The sun beat down bright and hot, the weather promising another scorching day.

Perhaps the town's people would blame the extreme heat on the witches, too, like they did every other negative thing that happened. She rolled her eyes and headed toward the café doors.

A panicked holler from across the street caused her to jerk around.

A teenage boy wearing a ball cap and jeans flew down the sidewalk on his skateboard, traveling much too fast for the downtown cobblestone sidewalks. She opened her mouth to yell for him to slow down, but he jumped off the skateboard, dropped and rolled like someone abandoning a car with no brakes.

A second later, he was back on his feet and dashed inside the hardware store.

She stared bewildered at the abandoned skateboard that continued down the street until it rolled off into the grass.

She was about to chalk it up to crazy teenage antics, but a swarm of bees swooped in, following the same path. With a frenzied swirl, they covered the kid's skateboard as though they were hell-bent on murdering it.

She hoped the kid, whatever he'd done to make the bees mad, had learned his lesson. Bees might be small, but the Blessed Mother had gifted them with nasty weapons.

Hazel pulled open the door to the diner and inhaled the lovely, cool air as she stepped inside.

"Morning, Haze," Cora called from behind the counter where she refilled dear Mr. Fletcher's coffee cup. Cora's warm smile creased her cheeks and left her looking more like a twenty-five-year old than a woman in her thirties.

"Hey, Cora." Hazel strode forward and glanced about the restaurant. "Margaret here yet?"

Cora shook her head, her blond ponytail swinging. "Not yet. Are you meeting for breakfast or early lunch?"

Hazel slid onto the brown leather counter stool. "No, we're headed into Salem."

Cora's aura brightened. "That sounds fun. I'm sure Margaret could use it to counter the stress she's been under with her sister."

She propped her elbows on the counter and glanced once at Mr. Fletcher. The senile old man was preoccupied pouring massive amounts of sugar and cream into his cup.

She turned back to Cora and leaned close to whisper. "We're going to investigate one of the bridezillas who was at Fiona's wedding."

Cora laughed and shook her head. "Peter won't like that."

"Actually, it was his idea."

She lifted her brows in surprise. "Seriously? What brought about that change?"

Hazel snickered. "The fact that he can't handle a crying female. Every time he tries to interview Sondra about the details of her previous relationship with the groom and what transpired afterward, she cries too hard to finish a sentence."

"Do you and Margaret think you'll fare any better?"

Hazel flashed her a sarcastic look. "We're women with feelings. What do you think?"

Cora chuckled. "Shouldn't have asked."

Hazel thumbed over her shoulder to the café's door. "Just saw the weirdest thing outside. Angry bees were chasing some kid on his skateboard. He escaped with his life inside Elmer's."

She froze. "Oh, no. Not the bees."

Cora had said that like they were a thing, not some random event. "The bees?"

"I really thought since Glenys had been the one to murder Belinda, because they are both witches, that we wouldn't experience their stinging curse this time. No wonder it's been so blessed hot, too. You'd better start cranking out more iced tea because this will last a while. People will be clamoring for anything cool."

Hazel snorted and shook her head. "I refuse to believe Clarabelle and her friends are the cause of the bees and heat. You and the town can't blame every bad thing on them."

Cora shrugged. "Don't kill the messenger. But if you hear buzzing, I'd advise you to run."

"That is beyond ridiculous. My long-ago grandmother wasn't a horrible person."

Cora pinned her with a sharp gaze. "No, she wasn't horrible. She and her friends were persecuted witches with powers. There were those in town who sought to destroy their very lives. Think about what kind of person you might be in those circumstances."

Hazel let that sink in and sighed. She'd probably be the same.

Time and again, she'd tried to imagine what life might have been like all those years ago, but she could never truly know. On an average day, she'd known more comforts than Clarabelle ever had, and that didn't count any of the fear or horrific events she'd watched and survived. "Why didn't you tell me about the bee curse? For that matter, how many other curses are out there?"

Cora widened her eyes in frustration. "I'm not even sure I know all of them. But this one goes something like, if a witch is ever killed in Stonebridge again, starting on the next full moon, the Blessed Mother's sting will find them wherever the townsfolk go. In winter, the freezing temperatures will be cold enough to burn. Otherwise, the sun will scorch the earth and the people upon it. In addition, they'll also feel the sting of the killer bees."

"Bees don't kill most people."

She lifted a non-committal shoulder. "Again, you're talking about today's world. Imagine having to survive extreme heat without good shelter and air conditioning. Imagine trying to escape a swarm of bees if you were out walking the road between your house and town. Most can stand one bee sting, but a swarm of them carries a lot of poison."

This was more than she wanted to consider. "Never mind. I don't want to talk about it."

However, she would be checking the three spell books that she had in her possession for evidence of any such atrocity. "Besides, I've heard it's supposed to rain on the weekend. Hopefully all this nonsense will be gone by then before everyone can go crazy over it."

Cora rolled her eyes. "Uh-huh. Me, too. We'll talk on Monday, and you can tell me I was right." She shifted her gaze toward the door and lifted her chin.

Hazel turned and spotted Margaret making her way toward them. She almost didn't recognize her wearing a t-shirt and jeans instead of some elaborate outfit. She lifted a hand in greeting. "Hey."

Margaret smiled at them both, but her friendliness was only surface deep. Worry and fear churned below. "Morning, Cora. Hazel. Are you ready?"

She slid off the chair, exuding a cheerful attitude, hoping it would rub off on Peter's assistant. She understood her fears for her sister, but there were plenty of other suspects to consider besides Gwen.

"I'm ready and looking forward to learning more about Sondra. She certainly has plenty of reasons for wanting Fiona dead."

"Agreed."

They said goodbye to Cora and headed for the exit. Hazel pulled open the door and peeked out for a quick bee check before she stepped out.

"Everything okay?" Margaret asked.

"Yep. I'm good."

Hazel thought of not mentioning anything about the bees she'd seen earlier, but Margaret had lived in town her whole life. She could be a good source of information.

When they were seated in her car, Hazel turned to her. "I saw a swarm of bees earlier. I think they may have been chasing a kid who'd probably provoked them."

Margaret did a frantic search through the windshield around the perimeter of the car, alarming Hazel.

"Have you ever seen anything like that before?"

Margaret groaned as though reflecting on a bad memory. "Oh, yeah. They got me good a couple of years ago. Peter, too, at the same time. We were attempting to rescue a little girl, and they turned on us."

"That sounds really scary." Like terrifying.

"Oh, it was. Peter took the worst of it. Ended up in the emergency room. There were other attacks, too. We called them killer bees though I don't think that was ever documented."

It made her sick to think her grandmother could be capable of such things. These people didn't deserve her wrath. "How long ago was that?"

Margaret squinted as though that would help her recall. "That would have been... Oh, yes. Not long after Sarah had her tragic accident. I remember distinctly how fierce Peter had been to save the little girl, and I'd wondered if his loss of Sarah had affected that."

She could see that being the case. "Maybe so."

"Not that he wouldn't have saved her. But, he had a different demeanor after Sarah's death. Has ever since."

Hazel started her car and pulled onto the street. She considered researching old newspapers to see if there was mention of the event and if it coincided with Sarah's death, but she had a feeling it would only confirm what she knew in her soul.

Her ancient grandmother was a vengeful person.

And she'd be having a word with her about that.

CHAPTER SEVEN

Hazel pulled into the parking lot of a small strip of stores on the outskirts of Salem. When she spotted an empty space beneath a shade tree, she made a beeline for it and claimed victory when she slid into the stall.

She and Margaret exited the car and fell in step together.

"You know," Margaret said. "I never liked Fiona, and I always thought life would be better if she wasn't around. I was wrong."

Life loved to throw in surprises. "I guess I should be grateful I didn't know her much at all."

She agreed with a nod. "So, what's our plan? Are we going to barge right in and start questioning?"

Hazel rolled her eyes. "Of course not, silly. Working for the police department, you should have picked up some investigative techniques."

Margaret waved away her comment. "Not my area of expertise. Give me logical stuff or ask me to organize, and I'm all over it. I never was much good at creative, on-the-spot things."

She snorted. "I disagree. Some of those outfits you put together are darned creative."

Margaret grinned. "They drive Peter crazy."

She mirrored her expression. "It's good for him."

Hazel glanced at her friend as they stepped onto the sidewalk outside the small antique store. "Don't worry about anything. Just follow my lead."

The scent of weathered history assaulted Hazel's senses as she took in the mishmash of trinkets and old furniture. She'd been in some fabulous antique stores in her time, but this one wasn't half bad.

Since they didn't immediately spot Sondra or anyone who could assist them, they wandered through the displays, stopping to look at a few pieces of old jewelry. Hazel tapped the glass in a display case. "Look at this brooch. It's a little flower made from pearls."

Margaret widened her eyes and made an oval of her mouth. "That *is* nice. I've been working on a nineteenth-century outfit and that would go amazingly well."

Hazel caught movement from the corner of her eye and turned as Sondra walked out from the backroom. A look of shock passed over Sondra's face, but she immediately turned it into a smile. "Look what the cat dragged in."

Speaking of cats, Hazel hadn't seen hide nor fur of Mr. Kitty that morning and very little of him the previous few days. He hadn't been hounding her about reading Clarabelle's spell book, either.

She had a sinking feeling the sneaky rascal was up to something.

She pushed him from her mind and refocused on the current task. "Hi, Sondra. I hope that you don't mind that we dropped by."

"Yes," Margaret agreed. "After hearing about your interesting shop at the wedding, we thought it might be fun to stop by while we're in Salem."

So much for not knowing what to say.

Hazel tamed a snicker. "Plus, we wanted to see how you're holding up."

Sondra paused and then exhaled a deep sigh. "Well, I can't say it's been pleasant being the suspect in a murder case, but I'm not too worried since I'm innocent."

She also wasn't a crying mess like Peter had said she'd been with him. "That's good, and this place is fabulous."

A warm blush spilled over Sondra's complexion. "Thank you. Not everyone appreciates antiques, but they are my passion. And I do love to share with others."

Margaret pointed toward the pearl brooch. "If you came down thirty on the price of that brooch, I'll take it off your hands."

Sondra strode closer and slipped off the set of keys dangling from her wrist. She unlocked the case, pulled out the brooch, and handed it to Margaret to inspect. "Early nineteenth century. It's a forget-me-not split pearl brooch. The center is a tiny black garnet. As you can see, it's been preserved well. I should probably charge more than I am."

Sondra tilted her head from side to side while looking at it in Margaret's hand. "I could give it to you for...ten dollars off, but no less."

Margaret hesitated for a long moment. Hazel could sense her uncertainty and thought she'd hand it back to Sondra. Instead, she closed her fingers around it. "Deal."

Victory sparked in Sondra's eyes. "Excellent."

Hazel walked with them to the counter so Margaret could pay for her purchase.

Hazel studied Sondra as she clipped the string tying the price tag to the brooch. Her demeanor today compared to the wedding was significantly different, much more relaxed. "I'm really glad you're doing well, Sondra. You seem to have put that unfortunate event behind you."

Emotion flickered across her face. "I can't say any of it has been easy. I really loved Arthur, and knowing he left me for Fiona was unbearable for a long time. But, after seeing him at the wedding, I've realized he wasn't the man I thought he was. I'm grateful I'm not spending the rest of my life with him."

Margaret set her casual denim bag on the counter. "Sometimes it takes hindsight for us to see our blessings."

"So true. I'm embarrassed to admit that when Gwen suggested we get even with Fiona by playing some pranks, I felt like that might help me move beyond the pain. But now I can see it only made things worse."

Margaret flicked a nervous glance toward Hazel. "The pranks were Gwen's idea?"

Sondra nodded as she typed the amount into the cash register. "Something I'm sure she wishes now she hadn't done, like all of us. I mean, I don't regret making Fiona suffer some of what we did, but the way the whole thing played out was horrible."

Sondra paused and glanced between them, and Hazel's pulsed jumped. "Still, our pranks are a far cry from killing a person. You understand that, right?"

Margaret nodded and handed over her credit card, and Sondra slipped it into the card reader.

Sondra waited for the credit card slip to print and then ripped it from the machine. "There must be someone she hurt worse than us. Someone that she totally destroyed. You know, for someone to take her life."

Hazel had considered that, but she'd found the best suspects were usually right in the thick of things like the three bridezillas. "Or maybe one of your friends harbored more anger than you realize."

Margaret signed the credit card receipt with an angry flourish. "Gwen did not kill Fiona."

"Then maybe Carol," Hazel added, softening the blow.

Sondra shook her head. "I can't believe she'd do it. Either one of them, really. I mean, Fiona's antics have caused a lot of contention in Carol's life. She and her husband had to move in with her mother, and he's now moved out because he can't stand her."

That was a new bit of interesting information. "Is that so?"

Sondra lifted her chin in affirmation. "Carol refuses to live with him at his mom's where they'd have to share a twin bed and have zero privacy. Still, I don't believe that's enough to make a person commit murder. Do you?"

Margaret shook her head. Hazel did the same, though she'd found people had different tipping points. Some people could handle just about anything and not flip, while others lost their mind over words alone.

Sondra wrapped Margaret's purchase in tissue paper, stuck the small package inside a plain brown bag, and handed it to Margaret.

Margaret smiled, though Hazel could tell it was superficial. "I'm so glad we stopped in here today. It was nice to see you again, and I love my new brooch."

Hazel nodded her agreement. "You have a terrific shop."

A pleasant vibe emanated from Sondra. "Thanks. Come back any time."

Hazel refrained from saying anything until they were out the door and halfway across the parking lot. "What did you think of her? She seemed nervous to me, but that might be from everything that's happened. I'm sure she never expected to find us in her shop."

Margaret blew out a breath. "Well, first, I'm concerned that the pranks were Gwen's idea. That bothers me more than a little. As far as Sondra's demeanor, I didn't get a nervous vibe from her at all. Maybe a little reserved."

Or maybe Hazel had picked up on more because of her sensitive tendencies, which was often the case. "But not a murderer, right?"

Margaret stopped at the car door and waited for Hazel to unlock the car. "Honestly, Hazel. I don't think it was any of them. All three seem like decent people, if a tad stupid for their antics. I only came today to help you so Peter can mark all three off his list and get on with discovering who it really was."

"Yeah," Hazel said and sighed. That would be the best for all of them.

CHAPTER EIGHT

Hazel walked into the police station later that afternoon and found Polly McGillicutty seated at Margaret's desk. Polly's straight brown hair, no-nonsense button-up tan blouse and bland smile reminded Hazel just how much Margaret brought to this office. A woman in her late twenties like Polly shouldn't have the faded aura of someone on her deathbed.

Margaret might have said she annoyed Peter with her colorful flair, but Hazel would bet he'd prefer that light and energy over Polly's any day.

She stepped up to the reception desk. "Is Peter in?"

"Chief Parrish?"

The way she rephrased his name grated on Hazel's nerves like the scratch of a tree branch against her old house when the breeze stirred.

Hazel exhaled her frustration. "Yes. Is *Chief Parrish* in?"

Polly gave her a dull stare. "He's busy."

She could see that his door was open. "Busy?"

"Did you have an appointment?"

Hazel had no idea what she'd done to this woman, in this lifetime or a previous one, to make Polly dislike her. "I don't have an appointment, but he's expecting me."

Er...at least expecting her to give him an update on Margaret's and her interaction with Sondra at some point.

"I'm sorry. If you don't have an appointment—"

"She's fine, Polly." Peter spoke from the doorway to his office. "Unless I specifically say otherwise or I'm occupied with a serious matter, Hazel is always welcome in my office."

Hazel couldn't resist giving Polly a snarky look as she passed her desk.

Peter let her pass through the doorway before he firmly closed the door behind them, locking out the snooty-snoot.

Instead of sitting, Hazel turned to the man who'd stolen her heart. "We need to solve this case fast. If I have to see her every time I come here, you won't see me much."

"Come here, my little witch Hazel." He chuckled. "See what I did there?"

She rolled her eyes. "Like I didn't hear that a million times growing up."

He held out a hand. "Come here."

She stepped forward, and he folded her in his embrace.

She peered up at him. "Really, though. We need to solve it for Margaret's sake, if nothing else. She's ready to snap if one more person insinuates her sister might be guilty."

Peter dropped his lips to hers for a long, warm kiss before he released her and strode to his side of the desk. "Problem is I haven't discovered anything that makes me think it couldn't be Gwen."

Hazel dropped into her chair with a frown. "But nothing that definitively points to her either besides the pranks, right?"

"From what others have told me, Gwen publicly swore to get her due vengeance. She's told everyone she's certain Fiona purposely sabotaged her wedding, and her humiliation over what happened is strong."

Hazel placed an elbow on the desk and dropped her hand into her palm. She regarded Peter with a defeated expression. "Sondra told us today that Gwen was the mastermind behind the pranks. Before that, none of them really knew each other, but they've since bonded over the tragedy."

He tapped his pen on the yellow notepad on the desk and stared at her. She loved it when their gazes connected while they processed information. She liked to think it was some sort of magic at work, when really, it was probably only their attraction to each other.

Which, in a way, *was* magic.

So, she was correct in her thoughts, which pleased her.

Finally, he dropped the pen. "I did receive preliminary information from the medical examiner."

She widened her eyes as her pulse increased. "And?"

He grinned, and she knew he loved the interest she had in his line of work. "She didn't die from strangulation."

Now, that was interesting. "What killed her then?"

"A blunt object to the back of the head."

She kept her gaze pinned to his as she processed. "Any idea what the object might have been?"

"Looks like one of the bride's shoes."

Her gut twisted. "One of the shoes that Carol took and hid? The same shoes she was looking for when we found her in the kitchen?"

"More than likely. We found both shoes near the body. So, either Carol brought them back to the dressing room and bludgeoned her with one of them, or someone figured out where the bridezillas had hidden the shoes and veil and snuck them back to the dressing room, whilst also luring Fiona there, so she or he could kill her."

"That doesn't look good for at least one of the three ladies, does it?"

"Nope. And the fact that someone would also take the time to wrap the veil around Fiona's neck and strangle her after she was dead, also suggests an extreme amount of rage."

Hazel slipped a strand of hair from behind her ear and twirled it about her finger. "Maybe the killer didn't think the shoe had done the job and wanted to be certain."

Peter tilted his head from side to side, weighing her suggestion. "Maybe. Though you'd think if someone took enough time to wrap the veil, she would have been able to tell Fiona was dead. And checking for a pulse instead of strangling would take much less time."

He blinked several times. "I think the strangling was an afterthought. Like the killing hadn't been enough. He or she wanted to do more harm."

"That sounds like a seriously disturbed person."

"Agreed."

She stared at Peter for a long moment, trying to keep the small rip in her heart from growing bigger. "Margaret would know if her sister was that far gone, wouldn't she?"

He pressed his lips together, and she sensed the same worry inside him. "I would think so. But we'll have to wait and let the evidence play out."

She gave a soft snort. "I hate waiting."

He chuckled, and she was grateful the mood lightened. "I know."

She growled and then wondered what Peter would think of her next bit of information. "A strange thing happened today."

He tilted his head with interest. "Strange?"

"As I was headed into Cora's to meet Margaret there, I heard a kid hollering. I turned to see him barreling a million miles an hour on a skateboard down the sidewalk near the hardware store."

Peter shook his head in disappointment. "One of these days, one of them is going to get seriously hurt."

"No, that's not the point of the story. Just listen. When he reached the library, he didn't slow down, but jumped off and rolled to the ground. Within a second, he was back on his feet and raced inside."

"Was he goofing off?"

"At first, I didn't know what to think of it, but then this huge swarm of angry bees rushed by and attacked his skateboard."

Worry crept into his expression, and he scrubbed his jaw with his hand. "Oh, boy."

"Is that normal for around here? I've never seen anything like it."

He shook his head. "Not normal, but it has happened before. We had crazy swarms a few years ago. Lasted several weeks, and then they disappeared. I haven't seen them since. Some think we encountered a swarm of migrating killer bees."

Her heart sank further. "Is that what you believe they were?"

He shrugged. "Not sure. We asked the state to send an apiarist to study them, but the bees had gone before they could get anyone out here."

He absentmindedly rubbed his forearm. "I had a nasty run-in with them myself. If you do encounter a swarm, run, do whatever you need to protect yourself."

She hated knowing her family was the cause of the torment. "Margaret told me about you saving a little girl, and that they'd stung you pretty bad."

"If, by pretty bad, you mean I ended up in the emergency room, then yes. It was bad. I had over fifty stings."

She gasped. "Fifty?"

She couldn't imagine how painful that must have been.

A dark expression rolled over his face. "I'll just say I wasn't a happy man."

Empathy for his pain overwhelmed her. "Where did they get you?"

He snorted. "The question is, where didn't they? I was a swollen mess. Doc advised me to avoid bees. As if I'd gone looking for them. Only crazy people would antagonize the critters."

She considered telling him the truth. Witch-related topics seemed safer since she'd practiced a spell for him, unless it had anything to do with his wife. Still, she didn't feel she could withhold this information, either.

"Do you want me to tell you the theories I've heard?"

He lifted a brow and shot her an unhappy look. "Probably not, but go ahead."

"Apparently, the witches...my grandmother and her friends cast another spell on the town. Any time a witch is murdered, the town will feel their stinging wrath. If it's winter, the frozen temperatures will be cold enough to burn. Otherwise, the sun will scorch the earth and the people upon it. Oh, and they'll also feel the sting of the Blessed Mother's bees as an added bonus."

He rolled his eyes. "Or they're a swarm of African killer bees."

She bit her bottom lip, certain she didn't want to continue, but unable to not finish what she had to say. "When did this happen the last time?"

He stared at her for a long, hard moment, making her squirm in her chair. She recognized when he finally understood that she alluded to the correlation between his wife's death and the arrival of the bees.

"No."

She gave him an innocent shrug. "It makes sense."

"No. I don't want to think about it or consider it at all."

The mixture of pain and sadness on his face undid her. The fact that Sarah had withheld such important information from him must feel like a horrendous betrayal, made worse because he would never be able to confront her with it.

"Okay," she whispered.

She stood and made her way around to his side of the desk. Leaning over the back of his chair, she slid her arms around his shoulders and her hands across his chest. He was warm and strong, and she could tell he needed her so very much.

She placed her mouth near his ear, close enough that his hair tickled her lips. "I'm so sorry, Peter. I know this hurts you, and if you'd prefer, I'll not talk about it again."

He remained silent for several long moments, and Hazel wondered if she'd made matters worse.

She released her hold on him and peeked around front to see his expression. Sorrow shimmered in his eyes and bore a deep hole into her heart.

He pulled her onto his lap, and his mouth sought hers, giving her a desperate kiss. She wrapped her arms around his neck, and when he ended the kiss, she tugged his head against her breast and held him.

They remained that way until a sharp rap at the door startled them. The door flew open, and Polly stopped mid-stride, obviously thinking it was her right to enter without permission.

She widened her eyes and then lowered them into a look of disgust.

Without saying a word, she retreated and slammed the door behind her.

Peter released a heavy sigh. "She does good work, but man, is she hard to be around."

Hazel managed a light-hearted chuckle. "Gotta crack this case, I tell ya."

He gave her another long kiss, and then nudged her off his lap so he could stand. "I guess I'd better see what she needs."

She sighed, missing his body heat and the strong connection between them already. "I suppose."

Before she left though, she slid her arms around his neck and kissed him. "Call me later?"

One side of his mouth curved into a small smile, giving her hope. "You know I will."

Polly glared at Hazel as she left his office, and Hazel imagined pulling her wand from beneath a cloak that had magically appeared and casting a fiery spray of angry bees at her.

CHAPTER NINE

Hazel finished tidying the cozy tea station in her shop and glanced at the clock on the wall. Almost one in the afternoon already, and she swore most of her customers had come during the first twenty minutes of Gretta's lunch hour.

She had a feeling the dreaded heat helped her iced tea sales. Still, she wouldn't complain. A busy day meant a profitable one, and she was grateful when her business ran in the black.

The bell on the door chimed, and she glanced over her shoulder to see who'd entered. Gretta walked in, but she wasn't alone. Surprisingly, the town's dark-haired and blue-eyed bank rep, Lachlan Brogan accompanied her. Hazel's first thought was if Gretta and Lachlan had started seeing each other, Cora would be heartbroken that she never had a chance with her crush.

"Dang, it's hot out there," Gretta said, tucking her midnight hair behind her ear. "Look who I ran into out on the sidewalk on his way to see you."

Hazel picked up her dust rag and dropped it in the cleaning basket as she made her way toward them. "Hello, Lachlan. I've actually been meaning to drop by to see you."

His smile mirrored Gretta's. "I'll save you the trouble of inquiring about your home loan. We've reorganized the bank and finished processing your loan. All we need is for you to stop by and sign."

Excitement poured through her. "Really? Like it's mine?"

"We just need your signature."

She gave a small squeal, and Gretta joined her.

"This is so exciting, Hazel. I've always loved the looks of that old house and can't wait to see what you do with it."

Gretta's declaration surprised her. Hazel had assumed everyone would either think she was crazy to want to own it or think she was a witch. In all honesty, both were likely true.

Hazel blushed. "I'm sure it will take me a while to make it decent since it's been vacant for so long."

Lachlan lifted his chin to catch her attention. "I'll let you ladies celebrate. I'm meeting my uncle for a quick bite at Cora's and then headed back to the bank. Stop by any time after two, Hazel."

She sent him a warm smile. "Tell Luca I said hello."

Lachlan nodded. "Will do. It'll make his day."

"Well, good," Hazel said. "Because he always makes mine."

If she were twenty years older and not with Peter, she totally would have made a play for the hot Italian.

He waved goodbye, and Gretta turned to Hazel. "Have you thought of a theme for your house? Are you going to make the inside modern or go with an old-fashioned feel?"

If she was to live there with her grandmother's ghost, keeping an historic atmosphere would probably be best. "I think I'd like it to look much like it might have after it was built."

Gretta nodded. "I think that's smart. Others have tried to change it too much, and the ghost ran them off."

Hazel widened her eyes in surprise. "Have you seen the ghost?"

"Oh, no. I stay away from anything spooky, though if you lived there, I would dare visit. But I've heard many have experienced her." Gretta lifted an interested brow. "You've been there a few times, right? I mean you wouldn't purchase the place without looking inside. Did you see her?"

Hazel really hated to lie, but she'd found she had to skirt the truth on more than one occasion while living in Stonebridge. "I may have felt a presence there before, but nothing that scared me."

Gretta blew out a breath as she wandered toward the counter. "That's good. It would be awful to purchase the place, only to run out in the dead of night when you found a ghost hovering over you while you slept."

Okay, that did creep her out a little. She and Clarabelle would have a talk about respecting privacy and space. "I'm sure I'll be fine."

"Well, I look forward to hearing about your experiences."

Hazel hoped she looked forward to experiencing them and that this wasn't all a big mistake.

****

Hazel barely managed to focus for the next hour. Luckily, customers kept her busy. At two, she headed into the backroom and grabbed her purse.

"I'm going to the bank, Gretta," she called across the shop. "Call me if things get busy. Otherwise, I'm going to stop by my new house afterward."

"Sure thing, boss. Have fun."

Hazel's heart thudded in happy anticipation as she strode toward the bank. Halfway there, heat threatened to overtake her, and she swiped moisture from her forehead. This weather was becoming ridiculous.

As she neared the bank, an odd feeling crested over her like a dark wave. Prickles erupted on her skin. She glanced over her shoulder expecting to find a specter, but instead, a swarm of angry bees flew straight in her direction.

Son of a crunchy biscuit.

She released a yelp as she sprang into a sprint, running as fast as she could. She yanked open the first set of doors just as Quentin

Fletcher, sweet Mr. Fletcher's conniving grandson, was headed out of the interior doors. They met in the middle.

She put up a hand to warn him to stop as she wrestled to catch her breath. "Don't go out there. Bees."

He drew his brows together, peering at her as if she'd lost her mind.

After witnessing his belligerent outburst at Cora's not long ago, she'd noticed he'd avoided her at all costs. When he couldn't, his demeanor had been cold, if not hateful.

"I'm not afraid of bees."

He pushed past her before she could stop him and out the door just as the swarm arrived. She watched in horror as they surrounded him, and he screamed. He turned toward her with a shocked expression and yanked open the bank door.

A couple dozen bees entered with him. He slapped and yelped as they buried their stingers in his skin. *"Help me!"*

She swung her purse at several but didn't seem to do much damage.

Something sharp and painful bit into her forearm, and she gasped. Without thinking, she slapped at the bee and knocked it to the floor. She stomped the nasty bugger without hesitation and stole its life.

The interior doors swung open, and one of the female clerks peered at them with a startled expression. "What is—oh!"

She ran back inside, and Hazel followed.

Several men, including Lachlan, raced forward with fly swatters and rolled newspapers, yelling like heathens running into battle.

Five minutes later, all that was left of the bees was carnage on the floor. Several of the men sported swelling red welts, but they were satisfied with their accomplishments. They bantered about how they'd dodged one and chased down another.

Lachlan joined Hazel where she'd waited safely in his office and watched the epic Battle of Stonebridge play out.

"Did you see that?" he said and chuckled. "Total madness."

Madness was right, and apparently, all caused by her grandmother. "Scary, I'd say. You were brave to fight them."

"Best brawl I've had since college."

She'd never understand men needing to prove their prowess. "You have a nasty sting on your cheek." She touched her own to show him where.

"I'll be all right."

He took his seat on the opposite side of the desk and glanced over the papers in neat piles on the top. "Okay, then. Need to get my head back in the business game. Loan papers."

He might be fine, but the sting on her arm sent lightning bolts of pain across her skin. She dug in her purse for the small jar of soothing salve she kept mostly for dry hands, but the lavender in it might calm her body's reaction to the bee's poison, though she'd prefer a stash of plantain leaves instead. Still, the touch of magic she'd included in this batch might just do the trick.

She dipped her finger inside and rubbed a dab on her skin. Immediately, her pain level dropped to something more manageable.

Lachlan slid a small stack of papers across the desk to her. "Here we go."

She held the jar out to him. "I'll sign while you rub some of this on your sting. It will help."

He looked at it hesitantly before he stuck a finger in the jar and rubbed it on his cheek. A smile curved his lips. "Oh, yeah. Much better. Did you make this?"

She lapped up his praise like Mr. Kitty when she gave him warm milk. "I did, actually. Learning about tea has taught me a lot about the properties of herbs and other plants. It's just something I do on the side for fun."

She didn't want him reading too much into her special skills.

His blue eyes sparked with appreciation. "Maybe you should go into production. It's good stuff. Can't imagine you wouldn't make a bundle. The bank could give you another loan to get started. I might even invest myself."

Hazel chuckled. "I'm very flattered, but I have my hands busy enough with the teashop and buying a new house."

No way was she marketing something that contained magic.

He lifted a suggestive brow. "If you ever change your mind..."

"Thanks. For now, let's tackle this."

She turned her attention to the stack of papers and let him lead her through what each document meant before she signed. When he reached the bottom of the stack, he placed her copies inside a folder and handed the keys to her.

A huge grin split her face, and she folded her fingers around the keys. She owned her very first home. The place her long-ago family had once lived.

"Mine," she whispered.

"It sure is."

He gathered his stack of signed documents and tapped the edges on the desk to straighten them. "Congratulations, Hazel. Thank you for being so patient with us while we restored order to the bank."

She stood, unable to erase the smile from her face. "Thank you, Lachlan. It's been a pleasure."

Hazel was so happy that she almost walked right out onto the sidewalk without checking for danger. Luckily, the sight of a dead bee on the carpet between the doors caught her attention, and she halted.

She cautiously peered through the glass but couldn't see the dark swarm of death as she'd decided to call the bees. Her shop wasn't that far, but it was far enough, and she wasn't sure she dared to chance it. From there, she'd still have to make it to her house, but she did have her bike and could ride fast.

With Peter's warning firmly in her mind, she decided he wouldn't mind if she called and asked for a ride. His office phone rang without answer, and she could picture Polly checking the caller I.D. and then promptly ignoring it.

Next, she tried Peter's cell, but no answer there, either. If the bees hadn't just been outside, she wouldn't be nearly as nervous. Still, she couldn't stand there all day. She'd have to hope for the best and make a run for it.

She'd be fine.

Later, when Peter was free, he could meet her there to celebrate her new house. Before she dared a jailbreak, she fired off a text to Peter, telling him exactly that.

Just as she lifted a hand to push the door open, a dark-haired man with a super-hot Harley and a body to die for pulled up next to the curb outside the bank.

CHAPTER TEN

Hazel groaned. Why her? Why him? Quite frankly, Victor was a bigger nuisance to her than those darned bees. Except he didn't sting and leave a painful welt.

Forget that. He'd done exactly those things to her heart.

She pushed open the door, not sparing him a glance as she rotated and strode down the sidewalk.

"Hey goddess," he called. "Want a ride?"

She ignored him and kept walking as fast as she could, scanning the horizon for a dark and dangerous mass.

The motorcycle's engine revved, and she could hear him creeping up behind her.

"Let me give you a lift."

"I'm not your goddess, and I don't want a ride."

"I heard about the bees that were just here. Let me give you a lift. You've already been stung. You don't want one or more to get you again."

That caught her attention, and she rounded on him. "How on Earth do you know I got stung?"

The venom in her voice could have rivaled the bees.

He shrugged. "I know things."

"Are you having me followed? Am I somehow bugged?" She ran her hands through her hair, not wanting to think about the image of having bugs or bees all over her, whether real or electronic.

A wounded look crossed his face, and a twinge of empathy pinched her. She wished she could rip out her emotions like a wasp's stinger and stomp them, too.

"I didn't bug you."

"Then you are following me."

A suspicious smile curved his lips. "Might be keeping loose tabs on you, but I'm not following you. I just need to know that you're safe. Your mother expects me to."

Ugh. Why did her mother have to be in every awful thing that happened in her life?

"My...*mother* can mind her own life and stay out of mine." She used the word mother very loosely in that instance.

He opened his hands palms up. "Look, there are crazy bees circling the area. Someone saw them a few blocks down not long ago. Your mother would have my hide if I let them attack you."

The thought of running head-first into a swarm of bees frightened her, especially if she ended up like Peter with fifty stings.

"Get on the back of my bike. I promise it will hurt a lot less than those bees. Let me take you wherever you want to be, wherever you feel safe."

"My house isn't that far away. I can walk."

"You don't need to be afraid."

She wasn't afraid of Victor. She just didn't want to be anywhere near him. But the part of her that didn't want any more stings reminded her that a ride to her house would only take a couple of minutes. She supposed she could stand him that long. A few moments of torture would be better than the alternative.

She huffed. "Fine."

He grinned. "I love it when you get that fiery look in your eye."

"Stop with the creepy act, or I'm not going anywhere near you."

He looked wounded. "Creepy? I've never been creepy in my life. Women are thrilled to be around me."

"Only the dumb ones."

Victor jerked his gaze over his shoulder. The stiffness of his body put her on alert. "I hear them."

She gasped. "You can hear them?"

He kept his gaze on the road behind her. "They don't call me the most powerful male witch along the Eastern Seaboard for nothing. Get on."

Dang it. She sensed he might be trying to scare her into action, but then again, he might not.

"Now," he said with a more forceful tone that got her moving.

She hurried toward his bike, threw a leg over the seat, and settled behind him.

He revved the engine, sending a delicious rumble through her body. She did love a powerful machine.

"Hang on tight," he said and took off.

She resisted wrapping her arms around his waist for all of two seconds, until she feared she'd fall off.

The moment she touched him, something sexy and familiar reached out for her, and it took everything she had to block it.

The man's magic wasn't the only powerful thing about him, and she understood why he'd fascinated her younger self. That girl hadn't had much life experience and had sadly mistaken infatuation for love.

She couldn't be more grateful that she recognized that now.

Victor took the long way home, winding through the gorgeous tree-lined streets. If she could pretend the black pavement was dirt instead, she imagined that certain parts of Stonebridge looked very similar to how it had in Clarabelle's time.

She closed her eyes for a long moment and let the breeze make the heat of the day tolerable. Fresh oxygen infused her lungs, cleansing the life force inside her. She could certainly understand why people grew addicted to motorcycles despite the danger driving them.

Still, what should have been a five-minute ride had turned into fifteen. The longer she sat on the back of his bike, the more certain she was that he'd tricked her into riding with him. If he'd been so concerned with her safety, let alone his, he wouldn't be gallivanting all over town where everyone could see them including the dark swarm of death.

She'd bet her favorite citrine crystal that he'd had two motivations for offering her a ride. One, to be close to her in hopes of winning her back, which seemed oddly weird now that she thought of it. He couldn't possibly love her and break her heart like he had. So, what was his game?

Unless his narcissistic personality made it impossible for him to accept she'd ended the relationship. Maybe he wanted to win her back so he could break up with her.

She wouldn't put it past him.

His second and more obvious reason was to give Peter something to worry about and drive a wedge between them.

That wasn't happening.

Even if Peter did hear that she'd been on Victor's bike, he knew how much she despised her ex-boyfriend. He couldn't possibly believe that she'd give him a second chance and ruin things with Peter.

Memories of Peter's jealousy when he'd thought she'd been interested in Luca, the sexy Italian art thief, resurrected in her brain, making her nervous, but she pushed them away. So much had happened between then and now that solidified their relationship.

She nudged Victor with her thighs. The spike in his energy told her that hadn't been the best move. Next, she tapped his shoulder and leaned close to his ear.

"Did you forget where I live?"

He dropped a hand from the handlebars and placed it on her thigh. "Didn't forget," he called over his shoulder.

She groaned and shook her head. "Take me home, Victor. Now."

He didn't immediately respond to her request, and she wondered if she'd have to be more forceful. But then, he slowed and turned the bike back toward her house. They arrived in less than three minutes.

The second he stopped, she slid from behind him and turned an angry but mostly annoyed gaze on him. "That was not a ride home."

He lifted a shoulder and let it drop. "Haven't you ever heard of taking time to stop and smell the roses?"

"I don't want to smell the roses with you, Victor. When are you going to realize that?"

He grinned. "Oh, lovely goddess. Do you think I can't sense your attraction to me? Just now, while we were driving where the trees were the thickest and it was just you and me and the road...you can't lie about what you were feeling. Your heart chakra was wide open."

The man was impossible. "Open to nature. To the beauty around us. Not to you, Victor. Never again. I need more than you're capable of giving."

His expression turned serious. "I can give you whatever you need, sexy goddess."

Arguing with a man like him was pointless. "Thank you for the ride and your concern over my safety, Victor. But, I love Peter. Our souls have intertwined in a way you'll never understand."

Dark emotions blew in like a fast-moving storm, changing the energy surrounding them. "He's not meant for you. I am."

She was done with this conversation.

She shook her head and turned from him. "Goodbye, Victor," she called over her shoulder and headed straight into her house.

Inside, the cooler air calmed her head and her heart. She pulled the phone from her pocket and sent off a nastygram to her mother, telling her she needed to recall her henchman if she ever wanted to see her daughter again.

If she'd been speaking to her mother at that point, she would have called instead. But then she knew very well that would have disintegrated into another argument about what was best for her. Neither Victor nor her mother knew what that was. Only she did.

Peter was the best thing she'd ever had in her life. Period.

As she gathered a few candles to light and bless her new home and her supply of peppermint to chase away the spiders who'd taken up residence, she glanced about for her snarky cat. With as pampered as he was, she couldn't imagine he'd want to be out in this heat.

Still, he was nowhere to be seen. Even the food in his bowl from that morning remained untouched.

He could at least let her know if he had plans that would keep him away from home so that she wouldn't worry. They'd have a discussion about responsible behavior toward a roommate the next time she saw him.

She stopped and snorted a laugh.

Really, who was she to worry about a three-hundred-year-old cat? He obviously could take care of himself.

She grabbed her car keys from the table beside the front door and headed out.

CHAPTER ELEVEN

A weird sensation crested over Hazel as she pulled her car into the driveway of Clarabelle's house.

No, *her* house.

She'd always parked her car along the road closer to the grove of trees. If she'd ridden her bike, she'd park it alongside the house or in back.

But this time, she pulled square into the drive like she owned it. Because she did.

She released another tiny squeal of excitement as she removed the keys from the ignition and opened the car door.

Outside, she stared up at the house, seeing it with new eyes. It was no longer a place to sneak inside. She would fall asleep here every night and wake up in the morning with the multitude of trees shading her house and providing homes to the many singing birds. The gardens out back belonged to her now, a gift from the Blessed Mother passed to her through her grandmother.

The rental where she'd been living was small, but quaint, located only a few blocks from Main Street. She'd loved it there.

But this house was completely different. The two-story First Period home with adorable pitched gables had survived hundreds of years despite the curses her grandmother had put on the town including violent storms and extreme temperatures. Set amongst the trees and not far from a stream, it retained a wildness that called to Hazel like nothing she'd ever known.

Maybe that yearning was another of Clarabelle's curses. She couldn't know. Regardless, the feeling gripped her deep in the heart, and she knew it would never let go.

She'd finally come home.

Movement to the left of her stole her attention, and she looked just in time to catch a flash of ginger-colored fur dashing through the thick trees, along with something black if her eyes didn't deceive her.

The idea of Mr. Kitty having friends seemed odd, but of course, he'd want companionship, too.

She climbed the front steps with happiness resonating throughout her. The key slid easily into the lock. Even though she didn't really need it, she loved the idea of what the object represented.

Hazel stepped inside, and a rush of warmth and love immediately surrounded her.

I've been waiting.

She glanced about the room as though she might catch a glimpse of Clarabelle like some had. "Sorry. I should have come back sooner."

But, you're here now. To stay.

Hazel wanted to ask how she knew, but some things were better left alone.

"Yes. I've come home, Clarabelle."

A ringing of happy laughter echoed through the house. *Finally.*

Her grandmother's overwhelming exuberance left her guarded. "You've had other relatives in this house throughout the years, haven't you?"

She didn't receive an answer.

She waited a few moments but got the distinct impression Clarabelle had drifted off to somewhere else. Not gone, but not in her immediate presence. Perhaps she was off celebrating with her fellow witchy friends, if they still inhabited the earth somewhere in some way.

Whatever. She had her own things to do.

Hazel placed the candles on the mantle and lit them. "Bless and protect this home where I've come to be. Fill it with love and laughter, so mote it be."

She strolled through her new home, scattering peppermint near the doorways and opening all the windows to let out some of the stifling heat. The people of long ago lived with sweltering and frigid temperatures, but in today's society, she thankfully didn't have to.

She hated to mess with the originality of the house, but someone had added heat years ago. There was no difference if she had it cooled along with that.

As she glanced about the dusty, cobwebbed space, the magnitude of the work required to whip it into shape hit her hard. Her earlier visits had all been about the history and an overview of the rooms.

Now, she saw the dirt and the upkeep. When she'd told Lachlan she would be busy enough with her shop and this house, she hadn't been kidding.

Didn't matter, though. The house was hers, and soon, she and Mr. Kitty would make it a home.

Hazel took a seat on the top step and surveyed the charming rooms below her. If Gretta was still okay being alone, she'd start cleaning today.

But, first things first.

"Clarabelle?" she called out in a loud voice. "I need you."

A gust of cool wind flew past her, teasing strands of her hair.

"We need to talk," she said to the unseen entity. "The town has a little problem of far too much heat and a nasty swarm of bees, and it needs to end."

Death, came the ethereal whisper.

The heartache that followed the word burrowed deep into Hazel's soul.

"Yes," she answered softly. "Killed by another witch."

Noooo...

"It was all very tragic," Hazel conceded. "But neither party was entirely innocent."

The anguish inside her built despite what she'd told Clarabelle.

"I need to talk to you about the curse. Don't you think it's gone on long enough? It's hurting a lot of innocent people."

No.

Hazel flung out her arm as proof and pointed to the red welt that looked better since she'd applied the salve. "See? They're even attacking me."

Confusion circled the atmosphere.

"That's right. Whatever you'd intended didn't go as planned."

Hazel was encouraged by Clarabelle's silence. "The people who live here today aren't the same as the ones who hurt you and your friends. Many of them come from families far from Stonebridge who had nothing to do with what happened all those years ago, but your curse is punishing them, too."

Silence.

Then an angry energy circled her several times before vanishing, leaving an obvious void in the room.

Hazel sighed in frustration and then mumbled. "That didn't go as planned."

Though she wasn't sure what she *had* expected from Clarabelle.

An apology?

She tried to remind herself of the pain and torture her grandmother had endured and where her intentions had taken to seed.

Maybe Hazel wanted an acknowledgement or even regret.

Then again, from the pain Hazel sensed in Clarabelle's soul, she had a feeling not much had changed for her grandmother during the past hundreds of years. Maybe she was stuck living in those emotions, and that's why she seemed so unhappy and restless.

The sound of a car door closing stole her attention, and she hurried down the stairs, holding tight to the handrail lest she fall. She opened the front door just as Peter reached the door.

She strode forward and into his arms. "Hey there, handsome."

"Hey there, beautiful."

His lips covered hers, and she drank in the sweetness. Her life right now was amazing, despite certain members of the town who'd like to see her dead.

She dropped down from her tiptoes and took his hand. "There's something I want to show you."

Instead of letting her pull him inside, he remained rooted and stretched out her arm instead. He pointed toward the angry red bee sting. "What happened to you?"

She groaned. "I'll let you guess."

"Don't tell me it was the swarm of bees."

She nodded.

"Dang it. We've had four reports of instances today. EMTs transported an elderly man who'd had a severe reaction."

"I have to say, this kind of scares me, Peter."

One could stay inside while a violent winter storm passed, but who knew how long these bees would be in town? Life couldn't come to a grinding halt for weeks.

"I don't like it, either."

She braced herself for her next words, hoping he wouldn't think she was an idiot. "I had a conversation with Clarabelle about it."

His eyebrows might have lifted a bit higher than his usual questioning expression, but he didn't freak out. "And what did she have to say?"

"Well...communication with her is spotty at best. She tends to come and go, and never speaks in full sentences, but when I told her about all the innocent people her curse was hurting, she wasn't happy. More like confused. Like maybe this wasn't what she and her friends had intended."

She paused for a moment. "She didn't seem particularly happy that I'd been stung. I'd hoped she could help me find a way to stop it, but when I questioned her about it, she disappeared."

"Hmm..."

She waited for him to expound, but he remained silent. "Just, hmm... That's all you have to say?"

"What else is there? If you could find a way to stop it before they harm anyone else, that would be great. But it doesn't seem like Clarabelle will be a lot of help."

She sighed. "Well, I'm not giving up hope."

He drew a finger down her cheek. "That's my girl. Now, you had something you wanted to show me?"

She led him into the house, paused, and grinned at him.

He narrowed his gaze in a puzzled expression. "What?"

She spread her hands wide. "This."

"This?"

She wrapped her arms around his neck and peered into his green eyes. "Today, it's mine. All mine."

She didn't get the excited response she thought she would, and that made her heart ache. "I thought you would be happy for me."

He smiled then. "I am happy for you. I was just thinking about the future. Now, we both own houses. If things become...more permanent between us, where will we live?"

His question stunned her, and she temporarily lost the use of her tongue.

He gave a sheepish chuckle. "Sorry. Didn't mean to spring that on you like that."

She held up a hand. "No, no. It's okay."

Her heart thudded wildly, and she inhaled a deep breath. "It's...I guess I didn't think of that yet. I mean, I've been so worried that things won't work out between us, because really, they shouldn't."

He reached up and tucked a strand of hair behind her ear. His fingers left a fiery trail as he traced them down the side of her face and neck. "It might be too late for that. Maybe it's just me, but we seem pretty solid."

Love bubbled inside her. "We do, don't we?"

He placed a soft, lingering kiss on her lips, and she hated fighting reality when he released her.

"I'm not sure what we'll do." She lifted her brows. "You wouldn't want to live here?"

He chuckled. "I'd need Clarabelle's approval, and I'm not sure she'll give her blessing."

He leaned close to her ear making her shiver. "Do you think she knows how to mind her own business and not get in the middle of ours? If you know what I mean."

She rolled her eyes and chuckled. "I guess that could be a problem." Still, she wouldn't mind if it meant she'd have Peter permanently in her life.

She shrugged. "We'll have to see how it goes, I suppose."

He nodded, buoying her spirits that he didn't say no to her house.

She wiped her brow and chuckled. "It's really hot in here."

"Let's go hang out by the water," he said. "I know an easy way down the slope. You know, in case you twist an ankle or something."

She narrowed her gaze at his reference to the time when she'd been desperate enough to get his attention by pretending to be hurt. "I have no idea what you're talking about."

The smile that she couldn't keep from her lips suggested otherwise.

CHAPTER TWELVE

Peter held her hand as they crossed the shady street and then half-walked, half-slid down the slope that led to the happily gurgling stream. Cooler air wafted off the moving water, and that along with the shade dropped the temperature to a more bearable one.

Hazel breathed in the scent of damp earth and reveled in the transformations that took place before her. Leaves that had fallen the previous autumn lay decaying along the water's edge, the perfect example of life changing to death and then renewing once again. It was all an amazing dance that every living organism on earth did, whether they recognized it or not.

"I'm going to come over here all the time," she said. "The energy is amazing."

Peter's eyes flashed with happiness. "I hope you'll let me come with you."

Her heart flipped. "Of course."

He tipped his head to the left and tugged her in that direction. "You can follow this trail for miles alongside the river, though it's a rough path. Eventually, it will lead you to town."

"I might try that trek one day."

As it was, they walked until they came upon a large rock resting on the side of the bank. Hazel sat next to Peter, the coolness of the rock seeping through her jeans.

"Let me know when you're planning to move. I'll bring my truck. I bet Charlie Rossler would help, too. He's always looking for work."

She grinned, loving the way her man took care of her. "Maybe next weekend? I'm going to need a few days to scrub down everything first. No sense hauling clean stuff into a dirty place."

"True. I'll plan on it."

"Thanks. I'll check with Charlie later today."

She shifted on the rock so she could see him better. "So...you know I'm dying to ask, anything new on the case?"

He released a sigh that suggested she'd be disappointed with his information. "My guys have been digging deep, but not extremely. The three brides all appear equally guilty, but none terribly so. Not one stands out more than the others."

"Margaret won't be happy with that news."

"Tell me about it. I get a call from her every day asking what we've discovered. She made it very clear this morning that she expected better of us. I felt like I'd failed my history test and my mom wasn't pleased."

Hazel sent him a commiserating look. "Her sister is a suspect in a murder investigation. I think we need to cut her a little slack."

He lifted his hand in a frustrated gesture and pushed his fingers through his hair. She smiled at his mussed look and stroked the strands back into place.

Then she placed her hand on his cheek. "Have faith. We'll get it figured out."

"I'm concerned since I've had a hard time connecting with the groom. Arthur hasn't returned my phone calls or answered his door when I've sent officers. We had the landlord let us in his house for a well-person check, but the house was empty."

Her suspicions woke with a jolt. "Like he took everything and disappeared?"

Peter gave her a reassuring shake of his head. "No. More like he's gone out of town on vacation."

"Maybe he went away for a few days? To grieve? Some people need to get away from everything."

Peter exhaled and a grin slid across his face. "I should have thought of that. His mom has been avoiding my calls, too. Maybe I'll pop by and inquire if that's what he did."

He booped the tip of her nose. "You're so smart," he said teasingly, and she laughed.

"Have you considered Arthur as a suspect?" she asked.

"He's on the list, but we haven't found any sort of a motive. From what everyone says, they were very much in love."

She snorted. "For three months."

He smiled and nodded. "Yeah, only three months. But who can argue with true love?"

She grinned. Certainly not her.

Peter whistled and shook his head. "I did meet with Carol's mother. She's a nasty piece of work."

"How so?"

"Overbearing. Snide. Just downright rude. She corroborated that Fiona had swindled them out of ten thousand dollars. Fiona had taken money to pay for certain things for the wedding, but apparently, when Carol and her fiancé had to switch their wedding dates, Fiona told Carol and her mother that she couldn't get a refund."

"That's awful, but it does happen." She'd learned that with some of her vendors, too. Though not at that great of an expense.

"Yeah, except the venue said they did refund a good portion of the money. When Mrs. Yardley confronted her, Fiona denied the amount and said the small portion she did receive went to cover the charges for the extra work Fiona had to do to reschedule the wedding. Apparently, there was a long list of things like redoing the wedding invites and...whatever. I don't know that much about elaborate weddings other than they're a pain in the behind."

She chuckled. "But you had a wedding. Did you make Sarah do all the work?"

He eyed her with a sideways look, letting her know he knew she'd baited him. "She wanted to do it all. Said I was in the way. Besides, ours was a small wedding. I don't think it was much work."

She snorted. "Don't fool yourself. Even small events require keeping a detailed eye on many things."

He slid an arm around her waist and pulled her closer. "Why are we talking about my wedding?"

She squirmed but eventually leaned her head against his shoulder. "You're the one who brought it up."

"No, I'm not... Am I?"

She tilted her head back and looked up at him. "You're adorable."

He squeezed her tighter. "A grown man doesn't want to be called adorable. How about hot or sexy?"

His request brought Victor to mind, and she considered telling him about her unwanted adventure that afternoon. Then again, Victor wasn't invited to their party by the stream, so he could wait until later.

"You're definitely hot and sexy."

Pleasure rumbled deep in his chest. "Keep going."

She smiled at his playfulness and relaxed in his arms, perfectly content to sit where she was the entire day. "Umm...smart. Strong. Amazing green eyes."

"You like my eyes?"

"I love your eyes. It's the first thing that attracted me to you."

"Not this hot bod, huh?"

She giggled. "Oh, I definitely noticed the hot bod."

"We should get married."

She gasped and shifted so she could check his expression. "Are you proposing?"

He smiled and shook his head. "No. Not like this. If and when I do, it will be more special. But...what would you say if I said it could happen sooner than later?"

She realized he was serious, and his intentions shook her to the core. "I would say..."

Her brain fought to create an intelligent answer, but the dopamine flooding her senses left her dizzy.

"I would say that I would be honored to be asked."

He dropped his chin to her shoulder, and she could feel his breath on the side of her neck. "But you're not answering yes or no..."

She giggled. "Not if you're not officially asking."

He squeezed her until she gasped with happiness. "You are a tease, my little witch Hazel."

"No more than you, my sexy, hot police chief."

CHAPTER THIRTEEN

Hazel added sugar to the pitcher of refreshing hibiscus and lemon grass iced tea and stirred. First pot of tea she'd made in her new house, she thought and smiled.

She opened the refrigerator and placed it inside. By the time she and her helpers had been working for a couple of hours to move the furniture inside her new house, it should be cold enough for a refreshing break.

Then again, with the heat the way it was, they might need it sooner, in which case, she could pull ice cubes from the freezer.

She glanced about the kitchen trying to sense Clarabelle, though she hadn't once since she'd arrived that morning, and very little on the other days when she'd come to clean. She suspected she was in hiding, embarrassed over her curse gone astray.

"If you could turn off the heat," she said to empty air. "That would be really nice."

No answer.

Of course.

A knock sounded on the door and startled her. She glanced at the clock on her phone. Too soon for Peter and Charlie, though she did remember Charlie liked to show up early.

She made her way to the front door and opened it. Carol stood on her porch with a hesitant smile on her face. She'd tugged her hair into a ponytail and wore a tan polo that washed out her complexion.

"Good morning, Hazel."

"Carol, I...wasn't expecting you. I have movers coming."

"I know," she said, cutting her off. "Your neighbor at the old house told me and said I could probably find you here."

Hazel stepped back. "I can invite you in, but there's really nowhere for us to sit. Furniture won't be here until later."

She gave her a grateful smile. "That's okay. I won't take too much of your time. If we could just sit here on the porch for a minute, that would be great. It's shady."

Hazel sent a silent prayer of thanks to the Blessed Mother for the number of trees that surrounded her house. Otherwise, she'd be roasting.

She stepped out, and they both sat on a stair. The hour was early enough that the scorching temperatures hadn't come out to play yet. "Is there something I can help you with?"

Carol hesitated. "I'm not sure how to put this, so I'll just blurt it out. I think Sondra and Gwen are trying to make it seem like I killed Fiona."

Hazel opened her senses to get a feel for Carol's underlying emotions. Nervous. Scared. But then again, those could also be associated with a murderer.

"What makes you think they'd do that?"

She shook her head. "I can't say exactly. Just some of the things that the cops keep asking me. Like at what time did I take the shoes? Where did I put them? Stuff like that."

Carol inhaled a shuddering breath, and the stress she endured wafted out from her like a damp fog. "My answers never change, so I don't know why they keep asking unless they think I'm lying. And the only reason they would think that is if one or both of the other two have decided to make me the scapegoat to save their butts."

An odd feeling nudged her. "But Carol, those are both important questions to the case. I don't think it's strange that they've asked them."

Why on Earth was Carol telling her this? They weren't friends or confidantes.

Carol released a frustrated breath. "It's not that they've asked. It's that they *keep* asking. The same thing over and over again. Like they think I'm lying."

"I'm sure they're doing that to everyone. It's a tactic to see if someone will change her story."

She shook her head. "I don't think so. The worst is they also keep asking about my mother and interviewing her. She wasn't even at the wedding. Every time they question her, she rants at me all over again. I can't take much more."

Hazel remembered Peter's comment about Carol's nasty-tempered mother. "I've heard that your mom was really angry with Fiona, too. That Fiona took a lot of money from you."

"Nearly ten thousand dollars. It would have been the down payment on our house. Even though that money came out of Steven's and my pockets, my mom was livid. She keeps saying I paid for the wedding, and Fiona stole her money. That she might as well have flushed that ten thousand down the drain."

Hazel grimaced. That was a lot of money to lose. She'd probably feel the same.

"I told my mom that *she* paid for the wedding, and that the money that was lost was mine because the wedding still went on, but purchasing the house didn't."

Hazel did feel a genuine sense of loss from the woman and was sorry for that. "Did Gwen and Sondra know where you hid the shoes?"

She nodded. "We all agreed to arrive at the church early in the hopes that we'd have an opportunity to sabotage her. We discreetly kept our eye on the hallway by the bride's room. The moment it was clear, Gwen snuck in while we kept watch. She dumped itching powder all over the bodice of Fiona's dress before she stuffed her shoes and veil into a big bag that she had."

Once again Gwen seemed to be the mastermind behind the pranks. "Sondra said that all of this was Gwen's idea."

Carol tilted her head and drew her brows together. "Really? I thought it was Sondra's idea. Gwen invited me to join them for lunch, and we talked about how Fiona had ruined us."

She paused for a long moment to think. "It might have been Gwen's idea. I'm not sure. I know Sondra and Gwen talked first before they invited me to join them in their revenge. Three helping would make it easier than two, and God knows, I didn't mind making her pay for what she'd done to me."

The vehemence in her last words surprised Hazel.

Carol's face blanched, and Hazel figured she must have realized it, too.

"I was angry, Hazel. But not that angry. A person would have to be psycho to kill someone."

Or at the end of her rope. "Agreed."

Hazel glanced down the lovely tree-lined street and wondered when Charlie and Peter would arrive with the first load of furniture.

Then she turned her gaze back to Carol. "I can appreciate everything you've said. I'm sure you're under a tremendous amount of stress, and I can't speak as to whether or not Gwen and Sondra are trying to frame you."

Carol's shoulders sagged, and she nodded. "You're wondering why I'm telling you all of this instead of someone else."

Hazel scrunched her features into an apologetic smile. "Yeah, just a little bit."

"I really don't have anyone else to talk to. I don't have close friends, which was why it was so nice to have Gwen and Sondra to commiserate with. But, to be honest, I'd heard you're dating the police chief, and I was hoping you could put in a good word for me."

Hazel snorted a laugh before she could stop herself, and then regretted it when Carol's expression dropped. "Sorry. I don't mean to laugh. This is a serious situation. But Peter's a strictly-by-the-facts kind of man. I don't think I could convince him one way or the other unless I had something to back up my story."

"You could tell him you know me, and I'm a good person. That might help. And tell him my mother was nowhere near the church that day."

"So that she'll stop hounding you."

Emotion clouded Carol's eyes, and she nodded. "I'm barely keeping myself and my marriage together at this point. If something doesn't give, I'm going to break and lose everything."

Which didn't go far when Carol was trying to make herself appear that she wasn't crazy enough to commit murder.

Hazel gave her a kind smile. "I don't know if it will help, but I'll put in a good word for you and tell Peter what we've talked about."

Relief broke over her face, and she exhaled. "Thank you. Thank you so much."

Carol stood. "I'm sorry to have kept you so long. I know you're very busy."

Hazel stood, too. "Moving into a new home is daunting for sure."

Carol winced, and Hazel realized the mention of moving into a new house might be hard for Carol to hear.

She placed a hand on her arm and sent warm thoughts her way. "Hang in there. Things will get better. Be good to your husband and stick together. You'll make it through this."

Carol nodded, and a tear slipped down her cheek. "Thanks."

She hurried off after that, and Hazel feared the woman was in for a good cry. Then again, maybe that was exactly what she needed.

CHAPTER FOURTEEN

After Carol's departure, Hazel emptied more of the kitchen boxes she'd packed the day before while she waited for the men. Her phone rang, startling her, and she dug it out from beneath the box that held all her kitchen utensils.

"You're going to kill me, Hazel." Peter's frustration came across the line, pinging her anxiety.

"Why? What's wrong?"

"Just got a call on a large, angry swarm of bees that has Mrs. Lemon and four of her grandkids trapped in a small shed. With these sweltering temperatures, we can't wait for the bees to move along. I've got two other officers who are helping, but I need to be there. You know how dangerous those bees can be."

Oh, yes. She'd been unlucky enough to enjoy the sting of one of them.

She worried about his safety, though. "Are you sure you're the best person after what happened to you last time?"

His voice softened. "I'll be careful. But I feel bad that I had to bail on Charlie. My truck is half loaded so I left it at your house and walked to the station. He was going to see if he could find someone else to help. I'll come over as soon as I can."

"Of course. Please be careful. We'll handle things here."

"Thanks," he said with relief in his voice. "See you soon."

"Okay."

"Love you, bye." The line went dead.

Love you, bye?

Her stomach turned topsy turvy. Had he meant to say that, or was it just a phrase he'd used, perhaps with Sarah or his family?

It wasn't an actual declaration, but...

"Love you, bye," she whispered and pocketed her phone.

A grin pushed out her cheeks. Whether he'd meant it literally or not, she liked it.

Twenty minutes later, the sound of vehicles approaching grew louder, and she abandoned her task in the kitchen and headed toward the front of the house. Charlie had backed his truck into her drive, while Peter's sat parked on the road.

She pushed open the screen door and stepped out just as Victor exited Peter's truck. Oh, no.

No, no, no, no, no.

Peter was a decent, calm man for the most part, but knowing Victor drove his truck might send him over the edge. She marched directly for her ex-boyfriend.

"What in the Samhain are you up to?" she said with a vicious tone. "You need to hit the road right now."

Victor held up both hands. "Whoa, goddess. Chill out. I'm just trying to do a good deed."

Her heart thudded in wild beats, heating her blood and sending her common sense running for the shadows. "You're driving my boyfriend's truck. I think we both know how well that will go over. How dare you?"

Victor chuckled. "This has nothing to do with driving Peter's truck, though I admit it is a nice ride."

"If you don't get your sorry butt out of here, off my property right now, I'll hex you with a pox that will make certain parts of you fall off."

The grin on his face riled her even more. "Come on, Hazel. We both know you don't have it in you to do that. You're too kind."

She was feeling anything near kind right now. "I will—"

"Hazel?" Charlie called from behind her.

She turned to find him striding across the lawn toward them, and she swallowed the rest of her response. For now.

"Hazel," he said again as he joined them. "Did Peter call? I guess he has some emergency he has to handle."

Her pulse thudded loudly in her ears making it feel like her whole head vibrated. "That's what he said."

Charlie glanced between Hazel and Victor, oblivious of the raging undercurrents. "This guy was driving by and stopped to offer help. He's Victor."

As if Hazel didn't know that. "Yes." She turned a dark glare toward Victor. "We've met."

Although she wished they never had.

"Oh, good." Charlie smiled. "He totally saved my butt. I'd called my brother to help, but he's in Salem for the day. Looks like God was watching out for me."

More like the devil. Or Karma coming back for her.

One thing was abundantly clear. If she sent Victor away now, she'd be punishing Charlie as well. It didn't seem right to deny him the help he needed just because she had a personal problem.

Maybe a hard day's labor would be just what Victor deserved for meddling in her life. As long as she drove Peter's truck from here on out and didn't mention what Victor had done, things might work out after all.

Charlie clapped Victor on the shoulder. "Let's get the bed in first."

Victor winked at Hazel. "Let's do it, man."

She buried her nose and mouth in cupped hands and sighed her frustration. Why, oh why, oh why?

****

Three long, hot hours later, she watched the guys carry in the last of her boxes. Her phone rang, and she pulled it from her pocket.

Peter.

She strode to a shady spot on the lawn and answered.

"Hey, Hazel. How's it going?"

"Good." Something odd in his voice alarmed her. "Is there something wrong?"

He chuckled. "You're pretty perceptive. Just a couple of stings, but I'm all right. I was going to have John drop me off at your place so I could get my truck."

"It's here at my new house." He might say he was okay, but her heart told her otherwise. "Have him bring you here, okay?"

"Yeah, okay. Did Charlie find someone to help him?"

Blast it. He was not okay. "He did. All is well. Just get here safely."

"Will do." He hissed. "Ah, that smarts."

She wasn't sure if he was talking to her, to John, or himself. "Are you sure you're okay?"

"I'm fine. See you soon."

She hung up the phone and drew her brows together. She'd feel a whole lot better when she could see Peter's face and judge for herself.

Inside the house, she found Charlie and Victor standing in the kitchen, finishing off the last of her iced tea.

"I hate to push you out the door so soon after all your wonderful help today. But an emergency has come up. Thank you for everything. I'll transfer the money to you, Charlie, if that's okay."

He shrugged. "Sure. I appreciate it."

Victor studied her with a discerning gaze. "What's wrong, Hazel?"

Ugh. She just needed them gone, and she wasn't about to tell Victor what had happened to Peter.

"Nothing you need to worry about. Someone needs my help, so I don't have time to chat. Thanks again."

She herded them to the door and practically shoved them out.

A few minutes later John Bartles' new police SUV pulled into her driveway. Peter stumbled out of the passenger side, and his subordinate walked with him to the door.

Hazel hurried outside. The sight of many angry welts on Peter's pale face increased her concern.

"He said he was okay," she said to John and strode toward them. "He said it was only a couple of stings."

"I am okay," Peter said.

She ignored his statement and focused on John. "I think he needs to see a doctor."

John nodded. "He—"

"I've already been to the clinic," Peter said, cutting him off.

"They gave him a shot of adrenaline. Told him to go home and rest, and that it was a good idea for someone to stay with him for twenty-four hours."

Peter lifted tired but hopeful brows. "That fine with you?"

She snorted. "Of course, it is. Do you need help getting inside?"

He held up a hand. "I'm not dying, Hazel. I'm just wiped out."

"Thanks, John, for driving him over. I appreciate it."

He dipped his head in acknowledgement. "No problem. Get feeling better, chief."

Despite Peter's insistence that he was fine, Hazel wrapped an arm about his waist and walked with him to the door. He probably didn't need her help, but she needed to have her hands on him, to feel his energy, and know he was okay.

After they entered the house, she closed the door behind them. "Do you want to lie on my bed?"

He pointed toward the sofa that still sat in the middle of the room. "Couch is good. Just tired. Need a nap."

A whirlwind energy circled around, and for the first time all day, Hazel sensed Clarabelle's presence. She hoped Peter hadn't noticed, and that Clarabelle would behave and stay quiet for the time being.

She didn't need her grandmother's ghost interfering and possibly freaking him out while he was in that state. Peter had said he'd encountered her spirit before and seemed fine with her existence. But now was not the time to see if he'd told the truth.

"Go ahead and lie down. I'll grab you a pillow. I have a couple of fans boxed up, too, to give us a little circulation."

She dug a down pillow out of a box in her bedroom and gave it to him before she searched out the fans. She'd tried to label everything well, but she had at least twenty boxes with the tag "storage" on them.

When she returned with the fans in hand, he had his eyes closed. She quietly plugged them in and turned them on, and then dragged one of her chairs close to him.

He didn't open his eyes, but he held out a hand to her. She took it and gave him a light squeeze.

"Anything I can do?" she asked quietly. "I have some salve that helped when I got stung the other day. Can I put some on you?"

He sighed. "Yeah. That would be great. I'm trying not to be a baby about it, but this really sucks."

"Of course, it sucks. Bee stings shouldn't be taken lightly."

Instead of searching for the larger jar of salve that would be with her bathroom stuff, she went straight for the container in her purse. Each sting wouldn't take much, and then, if she needed more, she'd find the other.

Right now, she ached to give him some relief as soon as possible.

As she rubbed the salve onto his face, arms and hands, she counted the welts. "Sixteen," she whispered. "That's awful."

"I'm a tough guy." He shivered. "Salve is helping. I'll be fine."

Her gut told her otherwise. "Then why are you shivering?"

"Adrenaline."

He released a deep breath. "Don't worry about me. Just do whatever you were doing before I got here, and I'll hang out on the couch. Check on me in an hour or so."

An hour or so? That was way too long.

But, she was bugging him when he just wanted to rest. Even though it might kill her, she needed to give him space.

She stood. "I'll unpack my pantry stuff and see what I can fix us for dinner. You rest."

He mumbled his agreement, and his breaths grew deep and even.

She bit her bottom lip and slowly made her way into the kitchen. She supposed sitting and staring at him wouldn't help anything anyway.

After unpacking bread, pasta and many other things, she crept back into the living room. He didn't stir, but his breaths were even.

That was good.

Not knowing what else to do, she decided to go upstairs and find the bigger jar of salve so that she'd have it on hand.

She lifted a box from the bathroom floor and set it on the closed toilet seat. One by one, she emptied it, putting things in her new bathroom cabinet, hoping she'd remember where she'd put them later.

Clarabelle's presence grew near, but Hazel kept working.

Worried.

The soft word came from out of the ether, and she glanced about the room.

"Yes," she said in a quiet voice. "I'm worried. I hope you know those stings all over him are from the curse you inflicted upon us."

Her anger at Clarabelle increased tenfold. "It's not right."

A whisper of a caress brushed her cheek. *Help him.*

She glanced about angrily, wishing she could see the ghost face to face. "How? I've done everything I can."

A spell.

Her gaze darted about the room. "Are you saying there's a spell that will fix him?"

You can take the pain.

That was all the encouragement she needed. She abandoned her task and headed for the bedroom. Clarabelle's spell book was stowed in the corner in a box that she'd personally moved to the house.

She opened it and frantically turned the pages, trying to read Clarabelle's old-fashioned writing, searching for something that would take Peter's pain.

Here.

Hazel glanced up, not realizing Clarabelle had followed her. Pages of the book flipped and stole her attention. She did her best to keep her fingers out of the way.

When they stopped, she squinted and read the title of the spell.

Ailments.

She glanced over the ingredients. A candle. An amethyst. Rosemary, salt and lavender. Charred wood and white sage. Three drops of her blood.

Her stomach twisted.

She lifted her gaze and spoke quietly. "This is a blood spell."

Yes.

She swallowed, and her pulse pounded thickly in her head.

Do not be afraid.

She widened her eyes and glanced about, looking for someone to chastise. "I am afraid. Blood spells are dangerous, and I don't want to mess with them."

Help him.

She groaned her frustration. With a simple act, she could relieve Peter of his pain, and she was considering refusing him that. How could she say she loved him and let him suffer?

If she asked him, she knew he'd do it for her.

"If I do this, will it have any lasting effects for us or anyone else?" she whispered.

No.

Son of a crunchy biscuit. It appeared the fates had made it too hard to say no this time.

She consoled herself by remembering the tiny blood spell she'd done for money. No harm had come from that, and she'd made five bucks.

Clarabelle had assured her this one would be okay, too.

She pulled her suitcase from behind a stack of boxes and opened the secret compartment inside. She lifted a blue healing candle and a jar of small pieces of charred wood. Then she removed an amethyst from her box of crystals.

Lastly, she unsheathed the ruby encrusted altar knife she'd discovered in a shop in Boston when she was sixteen and had hidden from her mother.

The rest of the ingredients would be in her kitchen.

The first spell in her new house.

What a way to christen it.

CHAPTER FIFTEEN

Hazel arranged the items on a tray and carried it into the living room. As quietly as she could so she wouldn't wake Peter, she lit the candle. She opened the jars of dried lavender and rosemary and sprinkled a pinch of each on Peter's head. Tiny pieces of dark green and purple decorated his dark hair. She followed with a pinch of salt.

She set that aside and opened another jar where she kept small chunks of burnt wood. Her insides shook with the ferocity of an aspen leaf in gale force winds, and she prayed to the Blessed Mother to bless and protect both Peter and her.

She selected one of the charred pieces and dragged it across her palm where she would make the cut. Gently, she set the amethyst on the center of his chest, ensuring it didn't slide when he inhaled.

Then she set another match to the bound bunch of white sage until it caught fire. After a moment, she blew out the flame and watched as tendrils of smoke rose from the smoldering bundle.

The scent of burning sage rose to greet her, both calming her, because it reminded her of her mother when she'd cleaned the house, and terrified her, because of what she was about to attempt.

This was no novice spell, and she couldn't afford to mess it up.

Clarabelle was also in the room, of that she was sure. She glanced upward, hoping her grandmother watched over her and would step in before she did damage.

Hazel waved the sage above Peter's body to cleanse the atmosphere of any negativity, and then she turned in a circle, creating a cloud of smoke around her.

Peter coughed, drawing Hazel's panicked attention. If he caught her, he would not approve.

But he remained sleeping and the amethyst remained in place.

Poor guy really did work too hard, and to have a severe allergic reaction on top of it. No wonder he was exhausted.

When she finished smudging, she laid the smoldering bundle of sage on a ceramic plate.

With a shaking hand, she picked up the ruby-encrusted altar knife. She inhaled a breath to steel her nerves and pressed the blade into her palm until it sliced a quarter inch cut into the skin. She winced as her nerve endings screamed in protest, and her bright red life force rose to the surface.

She exhaled and worked to steady her nerves.

Now for the words. "Search for the poison. Take from this man in need. Heal his body, so mote it be."

A shiver raced over her, and she dipped a forefinger in her blood and softly touched him between the eyes.

A jolt of energy surged through her and tensed his body.

She placed a smudge of red on both cheeks and one at the base of his throat. For the final one, she slid her hand beneath his shirt and touched the skin over his heart.

He inhaled a sharp gasp, and his eyes flew open.

Happy, ethereal laughter echoed around them.

Intense heat infused Hazel's skin and left her shaky. Her energy faded like air from a popped balloon, and she sank into the chair next to him.

He rolled to his side and sat up. The amethyst dropped to the floor. Concern rolled from him in waves. She wanted to reassure him that everything was fine, but she needed a minute to find the strength to speak.

"*Hazel? What have you done?*"

She held up a hand to keep him in place and struggled to take a full breath. "I'm fine," she managed.

Peter's gaze jumped from her to the tray holding the tools of her trade, to the curls of sage smoke still rising into the air. "*What...did...you...do?*"

Her breath came easier now, though she still felt drained of energy. "A small spell. How do you feel?"

He glanced at his hands and arms, and paused for a moment as though taking an internal assessment. "Better. Much better."

A satisfied smile curved her lips. "Good."

He left the couch and knelt before her, pushing her hair back from her face. A trickle of energy flowed from his fingertips into her, and she absorbed it like a parched man drinking water in the desert.

His gaze bored into hers. "You took my sickness, didn't you?"

"Maybe?" she whispered. She cleared her throat and worked to make her voice stronger. "I was trying to dispel yours. I should have known that energy would need to go somewhere."

He cursed beneath his breath. "Why would you do that? I was doing okay. I would have gotten over it."

She needed him to understand. "Because I wanted to help you. Because I..."

Love you.

She wanted to say the words, but fear held her back. They appeared to be on the right track, but she worried about the many things that had the potential to derail them.

"So, you've basically taken poison from one person and put it into another. How does that make any kind of sense?"

She shrugged. "Because I'm not allergic to bees like you are. My body can handle it better."

She struggled to straighten in her chair. "I'm feeling stronger already. I don't think it made me sick like you. I'm sure a lot of how I'm feeling is because of the energy required for such a spell."

He frowned and shook his head.

She inhaled a deep breath and blew it out. "Really. I'm quite fine."

He pulled her to her feet and wrapped her with a possessive embrace. "Don't ever do that again, okay?" he whispered against her ear.

She hugged him tighter and knew that was something she couldn't promise. "I'm sorry."

He leaned back and checked her expression. "I guess it's my turn to tell you to rest. How about you lay down, and I'll pick up some burgers from Cora's for us?"

That did sound amazing. "Okay. But you should wash off the blood." She touched her forehead and cheeks. "And there's stuff in your hair."

He brushed the herbs from his head and walked toward the bathroom. "What were you thinking?" he muttered.

A few minutes later, he left her alone lying on the couch with the fan cooling her heated body. Even though she'd accepted his sickness, she was doing a whole lot better than he'd been, and she couldn't regret what she'd done.

A skitter of excitement raced through her when she paused long enough to realize she really had pulled off that spell. For her, the results weren't what she'd expected. But for Peter...

An hour ago, he'd been flat on his back, passed out on the couch. Now, he was better.

A smile blossomed on her face. "I did it," she whispered.

Yes...

The sudden acceptance of that knowledge left her too tired to sleep. Instead, she lifted Clarabelle's spell book from the coffee table and took another look at the spell she'd just performed.

She'd completed it exactly as outlined. And it had worked.

Crazy, but exhilarating.

She flipped back through a couple of pages, grateful that she didn't need a spell to make a candle last longer or one to clear muddy water for drinking.

When she came across a stinging curse, she halted and widened her eyes. She'd noticed the title before, but there had been nothing about it to encourage her to read further.

Now, however, was a completely different story.

This was it. The spell Clarabelle and apparently her friends had used to create the stinging curse.

Hazel slowly whispered the first paragraph. "Whosoever shall kill a witch, will bring damnation upon this town. Whether it be the bitter sting of a harsh winter, or the sting of burning sun upon their skins, they shall pay. This curse shall commence on the first day of the next full moon and shall continue henceforth until the next."

Wow.

Like she couldn't exactly blame them, and in modern times, those curses were dang uncomfortable, but not often deadly. But back three hundred years ago? The townspeople would have lost many of the old and the young.

If they didn't freeze to death, they would likely run out of food because it would be hard to leave the house. In the summer, their crops would likely shrivel. Either way, animals would have perished, making it that much more difficult.

The curse was full of wickedness. What must her poor grandmother have suffered to be filled with such vengeance?

It hurt her heart to think of it.

A heavy sigh floated down on her, and she sensed Clarabelle was near. "I'm sorry for what happened to you and your friends," she said quietly.

Smothering sadness surrounded her, and she had to mentally block it before it dragged her under.

"The bees, though," she muttered. "Is that another curse? Not part of this one?"

Not meant to be.

"A mistake? Can the curse be undone?"

Nooo...

"No, it can't be, or no, you don't wish it to be?"

A forceful wind knocked her hard enough to surprise her, and then everything grew quiet.

She sat still for a long moment pondering what had just taken place.

If she had to make a guess, she'd say that yes, there was a way to undo the curse...maybe all of them. Quite possibly Clarabelle had exited the room in a literal huff, throwing a fit because she didn't want Hazel to attempt to break the curse.

CHAPTER SIXTEEN

Hazel drove into town late the following Monday morning. Fighting off Peter's poison had taken a lot out of her. For the most part, she was much better, but the task had drained her of energy.

Gretta had opened the shop, allowing her to have a relaxing morning before heading in.

As she turned onto Main Street, the sight of a kid riding his skateboard down the sidewalk wearing a Darth Vadar mask caused her to push on her brakes and turn her head to watch. Silly kid. Halloween was months away, and it had to be sweltering to have his face covered.

When she spotted June Porter coming out of the hardware store wearing long-sleeves and a ball cap holding a piece of netting to her head, she understood. The town's residents were protecting themselves against the bees.

She snorted at how silly June looked, and then sobered as she wondered if she should do the same.

Hazel parked in a small lot near her store since she couldn't find anywhere to park on the street, which made sense. No one would be walking about. Not with the bees and in this heat.

She checked for any dark masses that might be hovering in the air and then hurried for her shop and the safety it offered.

As she approached the teashop, her concern shifted from the bees to a new direction. Through the glass, she could see at least fifteen people milling about. Her shop had never been so full.

What in the world were they doing?

Relief broke out on several of their faces when she stepped inside. Mr. Peterson rushed toward her and peered from behind thick glasses. "Thank heavens. We were worried you weren't coming in today."

Several others agreed, and she noticed the groom's mother standing amongst them. What she wouldn't give to vanish the rest of them from her store right now so she could question her alone about her son.

She smiled at the group. She hadn't realized her store had grown that popular. "I'm sorry to keep you waiting. Gretta could have helped you."

Her assistant stood behind the counter and gave her a dubious look.

Krissy Farmer, a cute mom-to-be shook her head. "We're not here for tea. We need some of that salve you put on the guys at the bank. Lachlan said you made it with the herbs you use in your tea."

Uhh...that was true, but the salve she'd used that day also contained a touch of magic. "Oh, I see."

She didn't know how to disappoint them all, but she couldn't start selling magic-infused items. Not in this town. "I make it in small batches for my mother and her friends, and I don't currently have any extra."

Mr. Peterson put his hand on her forearm. "How long will it take to make some? I'll pay anything. My sweet Edna was stung eight times last evening, and she's a miserable mess."

"Calamine lotion might help."

Krissy shook her head. "Please, Hazel. We've tried calamine lotion and other things, and they don't help much. My two-year-old cries and cries. We need some of your miracle salve."

She swallowed as she glanced over the pleading faces. She couldn't deny these people relief for their loved ones. "Okay, well...I probably have enough stuff on hand for a little batch. That will give each of you a small amount to start with, but I can't sell it from the store. It would have to be cash or check, a friend-to-friend kind of thing because of regulations."

Words of gratitude filled the air, and one woman actually cried.

Mr. Peterson hugged her. "Thank you, Hazel."

She smiled wondering what they'd do if they knew what they'd asked from her. Would they still hate witches so much?

She walked through the logistics in her mind of what she was about to attempt. "I don't have containers for it though."

"What do you need? We'll get it," Mrs. Lemon's son, Tony said.

"Uh, maybe if you all have an empty pill bottle? That should work."

"Done." Krissy said.

The consequences of their request weighed on her. "Give me an hour. Bring your bottles then, and I should have it ready for you."

Mr. Peterson leaned close to her. "You won't sell it to others before us, will you? We were here first."

"Yeah," Krissy added. "Can we just pay now and pick them up later?"

The swelling need of the crowd overwhelmed her. "I'm not even sure what to charge."

Tony Lemon lifted a hand. "Will ten bucks cover it and give you enough for your trouble?"

"That's more than enough. I don't want to take advantage of everyone."

The crowd muttered amongst themselves and decided ten dollars was a fair price that they were happy to pay because she was kind enough to assist them.

"It's more than worth it to us," Krissy said.

Sounded like it was a done deal. "Well, okay then. Gretta will take your orders."

Hazel made her way through the crowd to the counter.

Gretta gave her an apologetic look. "Sorry, boss. I didn't know what to tell them."

She held up a hand and smiled. "It's okay. I think I can help them. I'm sure you heard that they're going to pay ten dollars for a container of salve. I'm going to get busy making it, and after they pay, they'll be back in an hour to pick it up."

Gretta grinned. "You're the best, Hazel. We all love and appreciate you."

Hazel smiled and shook off her compliment. They might not if they knew what she knew.

An hour later, Hazel had created a decent-sized batch of healing salve. She could hear customers gathering again in the outer area, but the mixture required the final, magical touch. She had to wonder if she was insane to perform a spell, no matter how small, right beneath the town's noses.

Probably.

She peeked out into her shop and found Gretta talking with several people. They all seemed busy enough and loud enough that she reasonably thought she might pull it off.

With her heart galloping, she lifted the mixing bowl full of salve and placed it on the counter in the back corner of the room. Keeping a watchful eye on the opening to the public part of her shop, she whispered healing words and stirred one final time.

The customary shiver of energy coursed through her, and she knew she was done. Pleasant sensations floated outward from there, and she couldn't help noticing how nice this spell was compared to some of the other scary ones she'd performed.

It was too bad life couldn't be happy with *nice*, and had to throw chaos into the mix instead.

With the mixing spoon and bowl in hand, she headed into the front of her store. Mr. Peterson was first in line. This time, he wore a baseball cap and had thrown the tulle he also wore over top of it to expose his face like a new bride waiting for a kiss.

She held back a laugh. "Looks like you've upgraded your protection."

He grinned and thrust an empty pill bottle toward her. "Got the idea from Krissy earlier. Works much better."

A good portion of the people in her store had done the same. Leave it to a woman to solve the world's problems.

She filled each person's plastic container and sent them on their way. Then another would step forward. She was happy to see Mrs. Wainswright had returned. The woman was toward the end of the line, but unless she hung about the store, Hazel would miss her chance to talk to her about her son.

Unless she could think of an unsuspicious reason to detain her.

When the woman approached the counter, Hazel smiled. "Mrs. Wainswright. Good to see you. Were you stung as well?"

She pursed her lips and shook her head. "My darned fool husband was. He'd been out to check on poor Arthur, and they attacked in the motel parking lot."

Motel parking lot?

Thank you, thank you.

"That's terrible. Which motel?"

Mrs. Wainswright widened her eyes as though she'd realized she'd said too much.

Hazel pretended not to notice and that her question wasn't a big deal. "I've been trying to track where the bees have been, so I know where to avoid. Although I suppose they can go wherever they want."

The woman relaxed a little. "I've been terrified to go anywhere since then, too."

Hazel scooped some salve and scraped it into the brown bottle. "Where did you say it was?"

Mrs. Wainswright waved a dismissive hand. "Out along the edge of town. I wonder how long the bees will stay and where they'll go from here."

She sent her a smile infused with warm, friendly feelings. "I'm not sure, but let's pray today is their last day in town."

Even though she knew it wouldn't be.

CHAPTER SEVENTEEN

The moment Hazel's shop cleared out, she pulled out her phone and headed toward the door. "I'll be right back, Gretta."

Her assistant's expression filled with concern. "Be careful out there. We should both get some of that netting, too."

"Definitely, and don't worry. I'll just be right outside the door."

The wave of sweltering heat nearly knocked her over, and she struggled to adjust to the change in temperature. She sat at one of her bistro tables beneath the shade provided by the awning, sad to see that her petunias had succumbed to the vicious temperatures.

For the life of her, she'd never understand how people survived without air conditioning.

She dialed Peter's office, and he answered on the second ring.

"Guess what," she said with enthusiasm coloring her words. "I found out where Arthur is staying."

"Tell me he's close by."

She sensed his excitement, and it added to hers. "Yep. He's close. His mother was in my shop and accidentally let it slip that he was staying in a motel on the outskirts of town. That can mean he's in one of two places, and they aren't far apart."

"Okay, good."

"So, can I go with you?"

He chuckled. "No, you can't go with. I'm not even certain how soon I can get away. I may have to send an officer."

"An officer? I didn't pass along this information so that one of your men could follow up. Peter, this could be important."

"Hang on."

She waited impatiently on her end of the call, and he returned a few moments later.

"Sorry. I needed to shut my door."

She chastised herself for her lack of patience. "Of course."

"As for Arthur, we've had a development in the case and could possibly be getting close to an arrest."

Her pulse jumped. "Who? How?"

He released a weighted sigh. "It pains me to say this, but it turns out one of the partial prints we were able to retrieve from Fiona's shoe belonged to Gwen. As you know, evidence leads us to believe this was the shoe that left the mark on her scalp and knocked her unconscious before the murderer strangled her."

He might as well have punched her in the stomach. "Oh, no. Peter, this will kill Margaret."

"You don't have to tell me that. Telling Margaret will be one of the hardest things I've had to do in my job."

He cleared his throat. "I'm gathering everything together and meeting with my detective team shortly. We need to get our ducks in a row, and then I'll send one of my men to pick up Gwen and bring her in for formal questioning."

"Today?" she asked quietly, making sure she could be available for Margaret to lean on.

"Yeah, likely today. We can't sit on it."

She nodded though he couldn't see her. "I understand. Will you call me when you can?"

"I sure will."

She hung up feeling as if she'd just lost a good friend. Chances were, when all was said and done, Margaret wouldn't care to see her any longer. Not as long as Hazel was with Peter.

A few seconds slipped past before she buoyed.

So, what if Gwen's prints were found on the shoe? Hazel clearly remembered Carol stating that she and Sondra had kept watch while Gwen had powdered the wedding dress bodice and snatched the other items. Of course, her prints would be on them.

She quickly dialed Peter's number again. When he didn't answer, she growled in frustration.

Fine. Let him meet with his men. They could talk to Gwen and maybe they'd even get more helpful information from her.

In the meantime, she'd continue looking for the real killer.

Hazel headed back into the shop. "I need to leave for a bit, Gretta. If more customers come wanting the salve, tell them I won't have any more until tomorrow."

Hazel strode through her store, picked up one of her basic teapots, a strainer, and a mug. Then she chose a sampler package with three different teas from the shelf. She placed them all on the counter in front of Gretta.

"Will you hand me one of our brown paper sacks?"

Gretta did, and Hazel piled her items inside. When she looked up, her assistant eyed her with interest.

"I have a friend who needs cheering up. I'll be back soon."

Hazel took the bag, hurried to her car, and headed toward the outskirts of town.

She slowed as she reached the Double Pines Motel. The Do Drop Inn was a quarter of a mile down the road. Both were meant to catch weary travelers who just needed a place to sleep for the night. A fair amount of Stonebridge residents used them as places to get away for the night without really traveling, or to house out-of-town guests that they didn't want underfoot.

She pulled into the parking lot and looked for the white Chevy sedan she'd noticed at the wedding that had been decorated with balloons and painted windows.

She straightened in surprise when she spotted it parked along the edge of the lot, hidden from view of anyone on the highway by a couple of tall pines. Hence, the name of the motel, she thought.

Flattened pink and white balloons were still attached to the windshield wipers as though they, too, had been murdered, and "Just Married" remained on the side windows.

Her heart wrenched at the awfulness of the situation. Such a tragedy.

She couldn't imagine what it might be like to have finally found Peter and married him, only to have him stolen from her before they'd had a chance at a blissful life.

She grabbed her bag of soothing teas and hoped they'd provide some comfort to Arthur Wainswright. She also hoped he might be able to give her more information that might help solve his wife's murder.

Twenty units stood before her. Ten on the top floor. The rest on ground level. Arthur could be in any one of them. She doubted the clerk would give out room numbers to a random person. Not with people demanding privacy these days.

With his car parked where it was, she would guess he was on the right side of the motel. He could be on the top floor, but there was only one other car in the lot, and she doubted the motel would make a guest hoof it up the stairs to the second floor if they didn't need to.

So, she'd start by knocking on the doors of the bottom five to the right. She was good at playing innocent and apologizing if she picked the wrong room.

No one answered at the first two. The third door was partially open, with a cleaning person's cart waiting outside.

She peeked in but couldn't spot any personal items.

She stepped up to door number four and gave a firm knock. She was surprised when she heard movement inside, and the door opened.

The pained expression on Arthur's face deepened. "I thought you were housekeeping."

"I'm sorry, Arthur. I don't know if you remember me, but I served drinks at your wedding. I knew Fiona"

He gave her a blank look and shook his head. "I don't remember much about that horrible day."

She could understand that. "Of course. I'm so sorry."

How could she pressure this man for information when he was so obviously in distress? He needed peace and time to heal.

She held out the bag of goodies. "I'm sorry to bother you here. I wanted to express my sincere condolences before you left town."

He took the bag and peeked inside. His gaze returned to her, and he nodded. "Thanks."

He leaned over to drop the bag on a nearby chair. Next to the bed, she caught sight of a silky black negligee lying crumpled on the floor.

When she looked back to him, she found him watching her with a wary expression. "Fiona's. I—"

He dropped his face into his hands and struggled with emotion. "It's all I have left of her," he said, his words full of anguish.

Oh, dear. "I'm so sorry to have bothered you, Arthur. I should go."

He nodded without looking at her again and closed the door.

She stood and stared at the closed door for a long moment.

Without him in her face, she realized something wasn't right.

He'd been sufficiently upset, all right. His words. His facial expressions. All in order.

But she hadn't experienced the anguish in his soul.

Nothing was there beyond sight and sound, and it should have been. Her gut warned that he might not be as innocent as he'd seemed.

She couldn't prove it yet, but she believed she may have just discovered who'd murdered Fiona.

She needed motive and how he'd accomplished it.

She needed to tell Peter and save Margaret's sister.

CHAPTER EIGHTEEN

Hazel parked as close as she could to the police station and then dashed from her car to inside. The second she spotted pickle-headed Polly still sitting in Margaret's desk, she frowned.

She was in no mood to engage in polite chitchat. "Chief Parrish."

The woman's lips parted in what Hazel would be hard-pressed to call a smile. "Not available."

Hazel glanced toward his open door.

"Not available," she repeated.

She huffed her frustration. "Do you know when he might be?"

She shrugged and gave her a sugary smile. "No clue."

If Hazel could, she'd jump over the desk and give her a clue.

"Hazel?" a woman called from Peter's office.

She turned to find Margaret in the doorway, and she motioned Hazel over.

Polly's snide expression dropped to annoyance.

"I'll just wait for Peter in his office." Hazel offered her own version of a saccharin smile and strode off.

When she reached Margaret, she didn't hesitate to wrap her in a hug. "I'm so sorry."

Margaret lifted her brows in question, and Hazel nodded. "I know."

Her friend's expression broke, and Hazel closed the door behind them for privacy.

She tugged Margaret toward a visitor chair and helped her sit. "Hey, it's okay."

She shook her head as tears rolled down her cheeks. "It's not okay. They're going to *arrest* her. The place I've dedicated my life to will arrest my own sister. I can't bear it."

Hazel grabbed a couple of tissues and shoved them in her hands. "Now, wait a minute. I know what Peter thinks, and I don't know what Gwen will tell him, but I have a couple of things that suggest someone else may have killed her."

Margaret sniffed and blinked wet lashes. "Tell me."

Hazel dragged a chair from against the wall and sat next to Margaret. "First, one of the things leading Peter to believe it might be Gwen is her fingerprints on the shoe."

Margaret nodded, and she figured Peter must have filled her in on that much.

"Carol came to visit me the day I moved into my house. I haven't mentioned what we talked about because it didn't cast Gwen in the best light, and, well, with the crazy bees and everything, life happened."

She grasped Margaret's hand. "Carol told me that when Gwen put itching powder in Fiona's dress, she also took Fiona's veil and shoes for the other two to hide."

Margaret's slow nods grew faster. "So, of course, her prints would be there."

"Exactly, and Carol can testify to that. Second, I discovered where Arthur has been staying and paid him a visit just a little while ago."

Hazel pinned her with a sharp gaze. "Margaret, I saw a black negligee on the floor of his room. He said it was Fiona's and made a big show that it's the last he has of her."

"You don't believe him."

She lifted another tissue for her friend. "At first, I was sucked in to his story, but then I realized I couldn't sense any anguish. For a man who'd just lost his new wife that way, he should have been more devastated."

Margaret's breaths came a little easier. "We have to tell Peter."

"We will as soon as he finishes with Gwen."

"I called her the day we came back from Sondra's shop and confronted her about masterminding the stupid payback stunts. Hazel, she denied every bit of it. I know my sister, and I know when she's lying. And she wasn't."

Hazel nodded in agreement. "I believe you. Now, we have to prove it."

They waited for nearly an hour before Peter returned to his office.

He walked in and then widened his eyes when he spotted her. "Hazel. What are you doing here?"

She gave him a sad smile and tilted her head toward Margaret. "Offering my support."

He blew out a breath. "Yeah. I'm so sorry, Margaret. We're not going to press formal charges this afternoon, though. My guys really put her through the ringer, but she stayed strong, and her story remained consistent. I'm going to let you take her home while we regroup."

Margaret's relief flooded the room. "Thank you, Peter." She turned to Hazel. "You'll tell him everything."

She sent her a warm nod. "I will. You go take care of your sister."

Peter waited until Margaret left and then closed the door behind her. He dropped into the seat next to her instead of claiming his office chair on the other side of the desk.

Frustration pulsed from him. "I knew this would be tough, but...man."

"Peter, listen to me. I tried to call you back after we'd hung up earlier because I remembered something Carol had said to me."

She spilled everything that she'd just told Margaret and ended with discovering the negligee on the floor. "Seriously, who would do that? If Arthur wanted to remember her, I can think of a million other ways, and if that's *truly* the belonging that meant the most to him, why would he toss it carelessly on the floor?"

Peter nodded thoughtfully and locked his gaze with hers.

She loved those moments when their brains were intimately connected and working together.

"We'll definitely call Carol back in to have her corroborate what you've said. If nothing else, that will buy Gwen a little more time. But I'm not sure about Arthur. You're going on gut instinct, but we can't arrest a man for that."

She really hated technicalities. "Okay, fine. I say it belongs to another woman, and you're doubtful. So, we need to prove it. The best way I can think to do that is a stakeout."

He snorted. "A stakeout?"

"Yes, exactly. You and me huddled in a car watching the motel tonight."

"I like the 'you and me huddled in a car' part."

She scolded him with a gaze. "Be serious. Gwen's future is at stake. We must watch him and see what happens. It could change everything."

He kept his gaze locked with hers and rubbed the scruff on his chin. Then he glanced at his watch. "Okay. One condition. You're bringing dinner."

She pretended to be insulted. "This is a serious police investigation, Chief Parrish. You can't put bribes on it."

He shook his head and grinned. "This is not an official investigation. This is me humoring you because occasionally your instincts are spot on."

"Occasionally?" she teased. "With that remark, it's doubtful I'll feed you ever again."

"A roast beef sandwich from Cora's with all the trimmings in return for you experiencing a stakeout. That's the deal."

Why did she bother to argue with the man? "Fine. It's a deal."

His lips turned into one of those sexy smiles that drove her crazy. "You grab food, and I'll pick you up in an hour. And don't get stung on the way home, or you'll ruin our whole evening."

She narrowed her gaze. "Funny."

Before she could come up with a good comeback, he tugged her toward him and placed a heated, possessive kiss on her lips.

She broke away when she needed oxygen. "Be careful, Chief Parrish, or I'll tell your assistant what you do behind closed doors."

He grinned. "Like she hasn't already seen it. But go right ahead. It might be good for her."

They both laughed.

CHAPTER NINETEEN

Hazel pulled into the driveway at her house. *Her house.* She still couldn't quite believe it. She gathered the boxed dinners Cora had prepared for them and headed toward the front door.

When she opened it, a flash of black fur dashed from the living room and into the kitchen. She widened her eyes. Mr. Kitty remained in the spot where the black cat had been and looked at her with an innocent expression.

She narrowed her gaze. "Do you have a woman in here?"

Geez. She sounded like a mom who'd just found her teenage son with a girl in his room.

Mr. Kitty lost his haughty posture and ran after the black feline.

She chuckled and then stopped suddenly. Did this mean she was about to adopt another cat?

She headed into the kitchen to put her and Peter's sandwiches in the fridge and saw no sign of either kitty. Didn't surprise her. That guy could pull a disappearing act better than anyone.

At least she knew why he'd been absent so much lately. She'd thought he would have been happy to live in the house with his current and previous kitty-mommas, but apparently, he had other things on his mind.

Anticipation of the evening's activities left her jittery. Peter might not believe her, but her senses, which were rarely wrong, told her Arthur Wainswright was not an innocent man.

She looked forward to proving that to Peter.

In the meantime, she had to wait. And she hated waiting.

She retrieved Clarabelle's spell book and sank into her favorite chair, determined to learn more about this bee curse. If a witch could cast a spell, then most times, another could break it.

Maybe if she looked long and hard enough, she might find a clue within the pages.

She made it to the middle of the book when she discovered tiny handwriting in the margin next to one of Clarabelle's spells. It was different enough from the other to draw her attention downward from the titles she'd been skimming.

A shoelace can be used in place of twine.

Those words were followed by the initials S. P.

S. P.?

She rolled the letters over her tongue a few times, and then paused. Sarah Parrish?

Then that would mean Clarabelle's tome hadn't been hidden all these years waiting for Hazel. It also meant that Sarah had no doubts that she was a witch. Especially if she was noting adjustments to spells.

She had to be more than a novice.

Hazel studied the writing again.

Yes, the style of handwriting looked modern. Definitely not something from Clarabelle's time.

She wished she could compare it to something Sarah had written. Perhaps when Peter arrived, she could ask him for confirmation.

If it wouldn't upset him.

Which it might because he was never happy whenever she'd brought up Sarah's deception.

She may need to ponder the idea a little longer.

The title of this particular spell, Fated Forever, didn't exactly tell her its purpose.

She scanned the content list, which included several personal items such as a lock of hair from two people and blood from both. *Of course.* Clarabelle did love her blood spells.

It seemed odd that it would require the blood from two, though.

A strand of twine to bind them. Or a shoelace it seemed.

Two rose petals.

Patchouli and yarrow. "This is..."

She frowned as she continued reading. "This is a love spell."

A love spell.

Her brain exploded with various notions, but they all led back to one thing.

It seemed dear, sweet Sarah had cast a love spell on Peter.

The implications of it and the extent of suffering Peter must have endured when her death ripped them apart blew her mind.

This spell would have made Peter fall deeply in love with Sarah, but it wouldn't have been of his choosing.

Peter might never have loved Sarah otherwise. She might have tricked him into giving his heart to her, making it the ultimate betrayal.

Then she reminded herself that she'd proven nothing yet, and to fling accusations at Peter's dead wife was a very bad idea.

She would like to think Peter could love only her, but that was selfish and unreasonable. Still, she couldn't help it.

If Sarah's betrayal was true, Peter had a right to know. It might even help with any residual grief he harbored.

And if he really had loved Sarah, this whole thing would be moot. No problem. No worries.

The sound of a vehicle door slamming startled her from her thoughts. She marked her spot and closed Clarabelle's book.

CHAPTER TWENTY

Hazel did her best to put on a warm smile to hide the crazy thoughts churning in her mind before she opened the door to Peter. She didn't want to blast him with her news and wait for the fallout. She needed time to process and maybe question Cora about the spell.

She exhaled and turned the knob.

He greeted her with a beautiful smile that charmed her to the core. "Hey, beautiful."

She grinned and allowed the happiness he generated to take over. "Hey, handsome. Are you ready for our stakeout?"

He tugged her to him and studied her eyes, a hint of teasing hiding behind his. "I think you just want to say you've done one. Like something to check off your bucket list."

He had her there. "What's wrong with that? Most people would jump at the chance."

"Not most people. But definitely you." He kissed her lightly on the lips. "Ready to go?"

"I'm so ready. Let me grab our dinner."

Removing boxed sandwiches from the fridge reminded her of another date, their first real one...that hadn't ended so well when she'd discovered a dead body.

Hopefully, this one would go much better.

The blues and purples of the evening fought the fading light to take command of the sky as they headed toward the edge of town. Every mile they drove stimulated her excitement.

Peter must have sensed it because he snorted a laugh. "You do realize that nothing happens during most stakeouts, right?"

Maybe so, but she didn't care. "Something is going to happen."

"You can't know that."

She shrugged. "I sense it. I sense the energy."

"That energy is all coming from inside you."

She gave a slight shake of her head. "Don't give me that. I sense it from you, too."

He dipped his head in concession. "Maybe so, or maybe I'm just excited to spend time with you."

She smiled but didn't respond. He might not want to admit the depth of her sensitivities, but she knew what she knew.

Peter slowed as they neared the Double Pines Motel. "Might be getting here too late. He might be settled in for the night."

Many more cars filled the small lot, making it easier to blend in. He pulled between a white pickup and dark blue sedan and rolled down the windows before he killed the engine. "It's hot enough to roast a fire pepper out here."

"Better than the middle of the day," she countered. "Besides, the bees should all be sleeping."

She removed her seatbelt and shifted in her seat to face him. "Have you seen the ridiculous things people are wearing to protect themselves from attack?"

He groaned. "All the ball caps over netting? Reminds me of a zombie wedding nightmare."

She laughed. "Better safe than sorry, I guess. I had a ton of people show up asking for my healing salve."

He lifted a brow. "And?"

"And I couldn't say no and not help them. But, Peter, there is magic in this blend. I tried adding some after you questioned me about it last time."

"Wait." He chuckled. "You're selling this to the town?"

She lifted her hands in a helpless gesture. "What else could I do? People are hurting, and customers are begging."

"I guess that's all you can do. I don't like the deception, but it is kind of funny."

She frowned. "I don't particularly like it, either. If this darned town could get its head on straight, then it wouldn't be a problem."

He conceded with a nodded. "How about we eat sandwiches instead of worrying about them?"

She pulled out their dinners and then pointed toward the motel. "His room is the second one from the end on the bottom, right side."

Peter shifted his gaze in that direction and then unwrapped his sandwich and took a bite.

****

She and Peter had long since finished their dinner, when Hazel released a heavy sigh. "Maybe you're right. It doesn't look like anything out of the ordinary is going to happen, and I've had it with this heat."

"Yeah," Peter said with disappointment lingering in his voice. "Unfortunately, that is the way of most stakeouts. They usually occur over a period of days, even weeks, before anything is discovered."

She was also tired of finding conversation that would distract her from thinking about the love spell she'd found in Clarabelle's book. She'd go crazy if she wasn't able to ask him about it soon.

She straightened in her seat and clicked her seatbelt in place.

Glare from someone's headlights washed across the dash, and Peter looked over his shoulder. "Hang on."

Hazel's pulse jumped to action. "Someone turned in."

"Yes," he whispered even though whoever was in the other car wouldn't be able to hear him. "Stay low."

They both scrunched in their seats as a red sedan parked a few spaces from them. A car door shut, and Hazel dared a peek through the passenger side window.

She sucked in a quick breath. *"It's Sondra."*

"Uh-huh," Peter mumbled. "That's a mighty short dress for someone going to console a widower. Especially one she used to be engaged to."

Arthur opened the door to his motel room, and Sondra slipped inside.

Hazel glanced to Peter. "Now what?"

"We wait."

She released an impatient sigh. "Again?"

"Just because Sondra knocked on his door doesn't mean either of them murdered Fiona. Maybe she's stopping to give condolences."

Hazel snorted. "Right."

He chuckled. "Look, you're probably correct in that there's something going on, but if we go knocking on his door right now, we're not going to learn anything."

She supposed he was right.

After thirty minutes longer, she couldn't stand it anymore. She pushed open the passenger door.

"Where are you going?" His whisper was harsh, which was why she hadn't asked for his permission.

"I'm just going to take a peek. See if I can see or hear anything."

"Hazel."

She shut the door and strode across the parking lot. A few seconds later, she heard Peter's door close, too.

He caught up with her as she stepped from the pavement onto the sidewalk. His fingers gripped her elbow, but she refused to be dissuaded. She jerked her head toward Arthur's room.

"We'll get caught," he whispered.

She grinned. "They aren't the only ones who can come to a motel for a lover's tryst."

Apparently, that convinced him because he released her arm.

Together, they slowly approached the room. Hazel crept past the window and casually glanced inside. The curtains were drawn, but a half-inch crack left her a tiny view. She crouched down and peered inside.

Oh, boy.

She gave Peter a wide-eyed look and motioned for him to join her.

Inside, the two lovers were locked in an intimate embrace. The black negligee or any other clothing for that matter were nowhere to be seen.

Peter gripped her arm and pulled her away from the window and back toward the truck.

Indignation rose sharp inside her. "Can you believe that? They disgust me."

Peter tipped his head in agreement. "Still doesn't make them murderers."

"You're kidding. It's obvious they've been in collusion."

He drew his fingers down her cheek and tipped her chin upward. "Honestly, I believe you're right, but we have to do this the right way."

"So, you're just going to let them go?"

"No." He smiled. "I'm going to call for backup before I approach."

The scorching flames of anger inside her died to a smolder. "Oh."

She waited while he called in to the station and requested a unit to respond to the Double Pines Motel.

Then he slid his gun from the glove box, tucked it into his waistband and turned to her. "I'm going to knock on the door. I wish you'd wait here."

She stared at him and remained mute.

"But you won't."

She shook her head.

"Dang it, woman. You'll be the death of me."

She certainly hoped that wasn't true.

"Fine. Just stay far out of the way, and if anything goes down, you seek cover. Do you understand?"

She smiled and nodded. "Yes, sir."

Together, they approached the motel room once again. Peter directed Hazel to stand to the side where she wouldn't immediately be seen.

Peter pounded sharply on the door. "Police. Open up."

She met his gaze and held it while they waited.

A few moments later, he pounded and repeated his message.

The sound of the lock clicking surprised Hazel, and she flattened herself against the side of the building.

The door opened, allowing light from the room to shine on the sidewalk. Peter pulled his wallet from his back pocket and flashed his badge. "Stonebridge Police."

"Is there something I can help you with, Chief?"

"We've been looking for you, Arthur. I'd like you to come to the station with me for questioning regarding the death of your wife, Fiona Wainswright."

"You took my statement that night."

Peter cleared his throat. "More evidence has come to light that suggests you might have something to do with what happened. I'd like you to accompany me."

Crazy vibes poured from the man, and Hazel wished she could tell Peter to be careful. On the surface, Arthur sounded reasonable, but his emotions were anything but stable.

"Now?"

"Right now."

"Let me just..."

Arthur shoved Peter, and he stumbled backward. He rushed past Hazel in a blur of skin and red boxer shorts.

Peter recovered within seconds and sprinted after him.

Hazel's mouth dropped open as they disappeared into the darkened trees. She couldn't very well go after them, but that's exactly what she yearned to do.

Shuffling noises from inside the room drew her attention, and she turned back. Sondra stepped out and then jumped in surprise when she saw Hazel.

They stared at each other for a long moment. Hazel sensed her urge to bolt, which spurted adrenaline through her own veins.

Sondra turned from her and ran in the opposite direction, but Hazel wasn't far behind. Hazel couldn't say she thought through the outcomes, but she wasn't going to let her get away.

Luckily, Sondra's heels slowed her down, and Hazel was able to kick a foot out and cause her to trip. Sondra went down, face first onto the hard pavement.

The sound of air whooshing from her lungs echoed in the quiet night.

Hazel wasn't sure what to do, so she did the only thing that came to mind.

She sat on her.

Sondra thrashed, but Hazel wasn't about to let her prize get away.

"It's too late, Sondra," Hazel said between deep breaths. "We know what you did."

Sondra growled. "We didn't do anything. It was all Arthur."

"You can't blame everything on him. You were in this together."

It was a total bluff, but Sondra didn't know that. "We have proof."

She squirmed and kicked her feet, trying to make contact with Hazel's back. "You have no proof."

"Your prints were on the shoes," she lied.

"They couldn't be. I wore gloves."

The second Sondra's admission left her tongue, she grew very still. Hazel wasn't sure if Sondra hoped she hadn't heard her, or what, but the cat was out of the bag.

"You're going down, Sondra," she said quietly.

Sondra's body shook, and Hazel realized she was weeping. "It was Arthur's idea. He said no one would figure it out. He said Fiona was the one who'd bewitched him, and that's why he'd slept with her."

"So, he really did cheat on you?"

"Yes," she cried. "She was planning our wedding and started hitting on him. When he found her naked at his house, he said he didn't realize what she'd done to him until it was too late."

Hazel snorted and rolled her eyes. Fiona was no witch. And Arthur was far from innocent in this matter. "I would suggest you tell the police everything you know, even if it further implicates Arthur. I can guarantee he's not going to try to protect you."

She cried harder. "He loves me."

"Oh, Sondra. If he loved you, he wouldn't have asked you to help murder a woman, no matter how awful she was."

Sondra dissolved into tears, but Hazel didn't relinquish her position until Peter's backup arrived. Hazel filled in Officers Larsen and Kennington on what happened, and Larsen took off in the direction Peter and Arthur had taken.

A few moments later, Peter, Arthur and Larsen emerged from the trees with Arthur in handcuffs. Scratches covered his arms, legs and torso, but she was certain his bare feet were far worse. She wanted to tell him he deserved that for running, but she kept her thoughts to herself.

The two on-duty officers loaded the suspected criminals into their car while Peter suggested the rest of the motel's occupants return to their rooms. "Show's over."

He took Hazel's hand and headed toward his truck.

"Everything okay?" she asked. "I was worried about you."

"All good. I just couldn't get him to cooperate even holding a gun on him. Every time I'd tell him to get up and walk, he'd run again."

"No wonder he was covered in scratches."

Peter opened the passenger door of his truck for her, and she noticed several red marks on his forearms, too. "Looks like you took a bit of a beating."

He snorted. "It's nothing."

She gave him a teasing smile. "I have some salve that will work wonders on those scratches."

"Another perk for having you as a girlfriend. I say let's go."

She glanced toward the police unit as it left the parking lot. "What about them? Don't you have to go to the station? While I was sitting on Sondra, she more or less confessed to murder."

He sent her a look of amused disbelief. "You sat on her?"

She shrugged. "You won't let me have a pair of handcuffs, so how else was I going to keep her there?"

He put the truck into gear and began to drive. "I don't know, Miss Hardy. I guess I should say good work."

"Thank you. Lucky for you, I have a small jar of salve in my purse, so you won't have to wait until we get to my house."

He took her hand and squeezed it. "Lucky, indeed."

CHAPTER TWENTY-ONE

By the time they'd finished with everything at the station, it was nearly two in the morning, and Hazel was exhausted. She'd nearly fallen asleep on the drive from the police station to her house. Peter walked her to the door looking as tired as she felt.

"Do you want to come in for a minute?"

He gave a soft snort. "If I come in, I'll end up sleeping here."

She shrugged. "I don't mind."

He tipped her chin up and kissed her lightly on the lips. "Okay, but just for a few minutes."

She knew it was selfish to ask that of him, but she wasn't ready to let him go. They'd had a great time together up until the point of the arrest, and she needed a little more of that before they called it a night.

Inside, she kicked off her shoes and curled up next to Peter on the couch. He wrapped an arm around her shoulders and held her close.

"I had a lot of fun tonight," she said in a soft voice.

His chuckle resonated deep inside her. "Leave it to you to have fun on a stakeout."

She nudged him. "Admit it. You liked it, too."

"Only because you were there."

She smiled. "Yeah, being with you was a big part of it for me. Though you did look pretty hot chasing a mostly-naked man into the trees."

He gave a snort of laughter. "Please don't phrase it like that in front of anyone else. It sounds disturbing."

She loved teasing him. "Fine, but you did look good all fierce and duty-bound."

He squeezed. "I bet you looked fierce sitting on top of Sondra. I'm mad I missed that."

"Oh, yeah. I was large and in charge."

"And you made her cry."

She shifted her gaze over her shoulder to look at him. "I didn't make her cry. Her choices and blindly following Arthur made her cry. Besides, her fire was back by the time she reached the station."

"She was belligerent, that one."

"No doubt. I'm glad Gwen or Carol didn't end up taking the fall."

He trailed his fingers up her arm, leaving shivers in their wake. "We always have to hope justice prevails. But some people get away with stuff their whole lives, and no one ever finds out."

Like Sarah with her witchcraft and love spells?

She tugged a strand of hair across her lips, mulling over what to do with her newfound information. When she reached the end, she grabbed the strand and repeated the action.

"What are you thinking," he asked quietly.

She gave a soft laugh. "What makes you think I'm thinking anything?"

He caught the strand of hair and wound it around his finger. "Because you always do that when you're thinking hard."

She nodded slowly. "I suppose so."

"So...are you going to tell me?"

She hated feeling torn between being honest and possibly hurting him. Strike that. She was *sure* her information would hurt.

"I don't know what to say."

He shifted until he faced her. "You sound like you have something serious on your mind."

She lost herself in his gaze, wishing she could find the answers there. "If you knew something important about someone, but also knew that information might bring pain to that person, would you say something?"

He stared at her for a long, hard moment. "Is that someone me?"

She bit her bottom lip and slowly nodded.

"Does this information have to do with Sarah?"

His question was a punch to her gut. She wanted so much to lie, to make up some random thing that wouldn't hurt him.

She took his hand and squeezed it tight. "Never mind. It's in the past and doesn't matter anymore. I might be wrong anyway."

"You can't close an opened can of worms, Hazel."

His phrase struck her as funny, and she wished she could laugh this all away. Unfortunately, she couldn't.

She sat for a long moment, frozen by her choice to bring it up.

"Tell me, Hazel. Regardless of the outcome, I deserve to know."

She gave a slow nod. "I guess you do."

With her stomach in knots, she retrieved Clarabelle's book and claimed her spot on the couch next to him. She opened to the page with the small notation.

She lifted her gaze and met his. "Does this look like Sarah's writing?"

He took the book and turned it to read it better. "I'm pretty certain it is. She always did that little curly on the ends of her g's and y's."

He drew a finger down the page as he scanned it. "What does this mean? What's it for?"

She inhaled. "It's a..."

Blessed Mother, help me do this.

"It's a love spell."

She swore all the oxygen rushed from the room, leaving her lightheaded.

He remained quiet for several long moments. "What are you saying? She cast a spell and made me fall in love with her?"

"I'm not sure," she whispered.

Anger erupted from him and echoed off the walls. "If that's true, then our whole life, our marriage was a farce. Is that what you think?"

Distress reared inside her. "I don't know, Peter. I...I could try to remove it. If that works, then you'd know for sure. It would also remove your heartbreak...if your love wasn't real."

The emotion in his eyes hardened, and he clenched his jaw. "Do it."

She swallowed and took the book from him. She'd already been studying the removal spell, wondering if it might work on the bee issue. But that seemed much larger than this.

A love spell, though potent, tied people together with thin filaments. With Sarah no longer in their sphere, breaking the spell would be much easier.

She gathered a white candle from her stash. With her stomach churning, she returned to the living room, set the candle on the coffee table, and lit it with a wooden match.

Then she turned to Peter. As she'd hoped, moisture had accumulated in the corners of his eyes. She lifted a finger. He flinched as she neared his eye.

"Hold still."

She captured a tear on the tip of her finger and turned back to the candle.

"A spell once cast, wasn't meant to be," she said softly. "Return the heart to its owner. Take this token of sincerity. Erase the lies, so mote it be."

Her hand shook as she held her finger above the flame. Heat rose and encircled her. Though she yearned to remove her finger, she had to wait until the fire had accepted her offering.

Peter slapped her hand away from the flame, and her gaze flew to his.

"You don't need to burn yourself," he said angrily.

She glanced at her reddened fingertip that was now dry. "It's done."

Peter clenched his jaw and shook his head repeatedly. He stood so abruptly that she nearly toppled sideways. "She made a damn fool out of me."

Her heart broke wide open for him. "I'm sure she loved you."

He pointed a sharp finger at her. "Don't. Just don't."

She stood. "Peter..."

"No. Stay away from me. I've had as much witchy deception as I can handle."

Her heart recoiled. "I haven't lied to you."

He snorted and strode toward the front door where he stopped and turned in her direction. "How will I ever know that? How will I ever be able to believe what I feel for you is true?"

He lifted challenging brows and then opened the door. He stepped into the darkened night and closed the door without a backward glance.

All emotion left her body, and she stood there for a long moment stunned. Then enormous pain rushed in like a rogue wave crashing against the shore, and her heart poured its anguish into a sob that echoed throughout the house.

She curled on the couch and cried.

Hush.

A soft breeze caressed her, and she slowed her tears.

She lifted her gaze to the ceiling. "I've gone too far this time. Hurt him too much."

Not your pain.

"No, but I'm the one who told him about it. I'm the one who ripped open old scars."

He will survive.

But is that what she wanted for him? To survive? The man deserved all the happiness in the world, and she would never be able to give that to him.

Hush, came the word again.

She shook her head. She wouldn't hush. Couldn't. There would be no consoling her heart.

She needed to end this thing between them, shred the fragile tapestry they'd woven, and set the poor man free so he could find a regular woman. One who wouldn't hurt him.

Her heart galloped in her chest, and she returned to a sitting position. She wiped a slew of tears with her finger and held it over the flame. Sobs broke some of her words as she repeated the spell she'd just used on Peter. She modified the very last line.

"Break the ties, so mote it be."

Her heart shuddered, and her soul quaked. Intense pain ripped through her chest, and her body began to shake. She struggled to breathe.

She may have just brought about the end of her life.

But the torture continued.

"Help me," she cried, hoping Clarabelle could hear.

Take it back.

Beads of perspiration broke out on her forehead. "What? How?"

On your knees. Beg for mercy. Take it back.

She rolled from the couch and onto her knees, gasping for air. "Please, Blessed Mother. Please. I take it back."

Again.

She paused as an intense shudder rolled through her.

"I take it back. I didn't mean it. Please, Blessed Mother. *I love him.*"

The pain in her chest eased, and she took an easier breath.

"Thank you," she whispered.

She dropped her head to the couch again and focused on her breathing while her body regained control.

When she felt strong enough, she moved to a sitting position on the couch. Regret seemed to be her word for the night.

She blew out the candle and reached for Clarabelle's spell book. Before her fingers reached it, pages flipped wildly and then came to an abrupt halt.

She lifted the book to her lap.

"The Fifth Curse," she whispered. "When bonded by true love, the tapestry between two shall never be broken no matter how much one wishes it so."

No ingredients for the spell. No incantations.

It was more that it was something already set in stone that perhaps the witches hadn't crafted. Maybe something handed down by the powers that be.

Whatever it was, the magic behind it was more powerful than anything she'd ever experienced before. These binds between Peter and her were unbreakable, and she'd likely die if she tried to sever them again.

Which meant she'd have to fix things between her and Peter or remain miserable for the rest of her life.

Who was she kidding? Either way, without Peter, she'd never be complete.

EPILOGUE

Four days had passed since Peter had walked out her door, and Hazel couldn't stand being without him any longer. She had to fix things no matter what.

She prayed hard that Peter would give her a chance.

For the first time in forever, the sun didn't scorch her when she stepped outside. She still opted for her car instead of her bike, just in case the bees hadn't left town with the heat.

A few minutes later, she strode into the police station determined to make him listen or else. When she found pickle-headed Polly still sitting in Margaret's spot, she frowned.

"Where's Margaret?"

Polly graced her with a dull look. "Excuse me?"

Her patience had left town days ago. "You heard me. Why are you still here, and where's Margaret?"

Her snarky smile fell into place. "I'm sorry. We don't give out personal information to just anyone."

Hazel closed her eyes and took a breath, afraid if she didn't, she'd do something she'd regret.

"Hey, Hazel."

She turned to find John Bartles walking up behind her. "John, hello. Is everything okay with Margaret?"

"Oh, sure. She and her sister went to Florida for a few days to soak up some sun and de-stress, as she put it."

Hazel cast a nasty glance toward Polly before she smiled at John. "Good to hear. I'm sure they both need it. Is Peter in?"

"No," Polly replied before John could.

Hazel ignored her and kept her gaze on John, waiting for him to answer.

John drew his brows together. "He actually hasn't been in for a few days. He's been under the weather with the flu or something. I'm surprised he hasn't called you."

Or something.

"Oh, you know how life can be. We're busy and miss each other's calls. I'll go over and check on him."

John nodded. "Good idea."

She drove the short distance to Peter's house, and tried to figure out what to say to him. She considered telling him about the Fifth Curse, but that might make things worse.

Maybe she should start by apologizing, but that seemed like she was apologizing for Sarah's betrayal.

By the time she parked in his drive, she hadn't come across anything that seemed remotely good. He'd been so angry, and rightly so.

But she couldn't live without the man, so something had to work.

Her pulse lurched with each step she took toward his front door. She whispered a quiet prayer and rang his doorbell.

When a few moments passed and he didn't answer, she began to fear the worst. But then the lock clicked, and he opened the door.

He looked like death warmed over.

His faded blue t-shirt had seen better days. The scruff on his chin looked several days old. But, the dark circles beneath his eyes, made worse by pale skin, worried her the most.

She reached for him without thinking. "Peter. Oh, my gosh. Are you okay?"

"Yeah," he grumbled, and she forced her way in. "I think I have the flu."

She was almost certain it wasn't the flu. He was likely still fighting their attachment and paying a hefty price for it.

If so, she could fix it. She slid her arms around his waist and placed her cheek on his chest.

When he hugged her back, she sighed in relief.

She stayed that way for several long moments, grateful that he didn't push her away. When she finally leaned back and gazed into his eyes, he seemed to have more color.

"How do you feel now?"

He scrunched his features. "Do you really think a hug is going to cure me? I mean, it's nice and all, but..."

She smiled, so unbelievably relieved that there wasn't a trace of animosity between them. "Tell me how you feel."

He paused as though considering. "Okay, maybe I do feel a little better. Please tell me you didn't put a spell on me."

Her heart opened wide. "Will you believe my answer?"

He trapped her gaze and held it long enough to make her heart pound wildly. "Yes, Hazel. I believe you."

Emotion flooded her, but she kept her tears under control. "If it makes you feel better, I tried to break the bond between us after you left."

Sadness enveloped him. "Is that what you wish?"

She shook her head. "No. I only wanted to spare you more pain."

He sighed. "It didn't work."

A heartfelt smile curved her lips. "No, and it won't. Like ever."

"Ever?" he repeated.

"It's the Fifth Curse," she said quietly. "When bonded by true love, the tapestry between two shall never be broken no matter how much one wishes it so."

He seemed suspicious, but it was only surface deep. "No one can break it?"

She snorted. "Well, none that I know of. You basically have two choices, Chief Parrish. You can love me and be fine. Or you can suffer while you wait for me to figure it out because I haven't a clue, and Clarabelle isn't talking."

He nodded slowly as though weighing his options. Then he stepped forward and pulled her into his embrace. "I guess I'll keep you."

The bonds between them wrapped her with love. "But how can you know for sure? I mean, I do, but you haven't been through what I have when I tried to break us."

He studied her eyes. His fingers were soft against her cheek as he brushed the hair away from her face. "That's where you're wrong."

She narrowed her gaze in question.

"Do you remember how you said if I was under a love spell that breaking it would ease my grief for Sarah?"

She nodded.

"It did. But it also opened me up to the fiercest pain because I'd lost you. What I felt for her was nothing compared to this."

This time, she was certain she'd cry. She wrapped her arms tightly around his neck. "Peter...I love you."

"I love you, too," he whispered before he captured her lips in a kiss that promised forever.

****

Read on for an excerpt from Book 6: It's All Sixes

If you enjoyed reading this book, the greatest gift you can give me is to tell a friend and leave a review at Amazon.

To leave a review, return to the product page where you purchased this book.

Scroll down to Customer Reviews.

Find the gray box titled, "Write a Customer Review".

Enter your review. Short reviews are appreciated as much as longer ones.

Thank you and happy reading,
Cindy

Excerpt from It's All Sixes
Teas and Temptations Cozy Mystery Series
Book Six

Glorious morning sunshine poured down on Hazel Hardy as she sat amongst the grasses near the edge of the dirt circle deep in the forest. She inhaled deeply, filling her lungs, and closed her eyes. Birds sang in the treetops, and peace resonated in her soul.

She couldn't imagine a more beautiful day.

Once upon a time, her ancestral grandmother had likely sat in this same spot. Hazel hoped at some point in Clarabelle's life she'd found happiness, too, and everything wasn't tragedy and fear.

Hazel lifted her arms and opened her palms to the sky, letting the universe's energy soak into each cell. "Thank you for your gifts this and all days."

She crossed her arms overhead, brought them down in front of her, and then drew her hands straight out to her sides. Energy rushed through her, creating a disturbance in the air. The birds in the trees squawked and took flight.

She smiled. She'd learned to do that as a teenager and had enjoyed it ever since. Before coming to Stonebridge, she'd often completed her ritual as a reminder of how connected she was to everything and everyone on earth. She couldn't agree more today.

A rustling noise interrupted her reverie. She panicked and flicked open her eyes. Mr. Kitty and his new friend, the black cat she'd seen around her house recently, darted in and out of the trees across the clearing, creating a ruckus.

Hazel relaxed her shoulders and inhaled a deep, calming breath. "Nothing but the cats," she whispered.

Mr. Kitty paused and glanced at her. He stared for a long moment, and then slowly rotated his head until he gazed south.

She followed his lead and then startled. Someone *was* watching her. Someone whom she didn't know.

A willowy woman with long brown hair that rested about her shoulders stood hidden in the thick trees. Now that Hazel had spotted her, she was surprised she'd missed the light pink shirt amongst the brown bark.

Their gazes connected for seconds, at least as much as they could across that distance. Hazel hoped the woman hadn't recognized her spiritual union with the powers that be.

The brunette turned and walked away. She didn't head deeper into the woods or out toward the road, but south, instead.

Hazel frowned. She hadn't explored far into the forested area in that direction, but, as far as she knew, there were only pines and maples spread out for at least a mile.

She shifted to her knees and then stood. If that woman could spy on her, turnaround was fair play. In all honesty, she needed to know who the woman was and her intentions. If she was an enemy, Hazel might need to mitigate damages caused by what the woman may have witnessed.

She brushed off the back of her jeans and headed south.

Hazel spotted the cottage before she came across the woman. The darling house wasn't big, but it held all the charm one could want from a tiny home. Gray stone covered the outside, while a brown roof topped it and yellow shutters hung next to the windows. Pink and purple petunias dripped from white window boxes, and a riot of bright pink roses climbed on trellises near the house.

She shifted her gaze across the lush property including the ivy-covered arch that led to a white picket fenced garden. What a lovely place.

The woman must have taken extremely good care of her plants

during the heatwave the town had just survived. That earned her more than a few points in Hazel's book.

A force of energy brought Hazel's gaze to the side of the house. The woman approached her but stopped before she came too close. A wary look hovered in her bright green eyes. "Can I help you?"

Hazel cringed with embarrassment. She'd basically stalked her and violated her privacy without thinking twice. If someone had done that at her home, she might likely put a hex on her. "I'm so sorry. I didn't mean to intrude."

The woman didn't crack a smile, and her demeanor remained guarded. As far as Hazel could tell, she didn't possess powers. But then again, she'd learned that those who lived in Stonebridge were masters of deception.

Hazel exhaled and tried again. "I just moved into the old house to the north, so I guess that makes us neighbors."

She kept her gaze pinned on Hazel. "I know."

The woman's aura was closed tighter than a rosebud, and Hazel wasn't sure she could ingratiate herself enough for the woman to open it. "Well, I won't keep you. I just wanted to introduce myself. I'm Hazel Hardy. I own the teashop in town."

"I know."

It appeared this woman knew far more about her. "I hadn't realized this house was here. It's lovely, by the way. A storybook cottage."

She gave a brief nod of appreciation but didn't respond.

Hazel lifted her hand in a wave and dropped it. "I'll just go then and leave you to your peace."

She turned toward her house.

"Wait."

Hazel glanced back, and the woman walked closer.

"I'm Anyanka Worley. Most call me Anya." She hesitated. "Well, my family used to call me Anya. The ones I knew well have passed on, so..." She shrugged.

A wounded, cautious soul, then. Hazel offered a friendly smile and held out her hand. "Nice to meet you, Anya. Being that we're the only two on this road, I suppose we should know each other. Of course, I'm always available if you need a cup of sugar."

Her stiff posture softened. "Thank you. Same for me."

Hazel glanced up toward the windows. "Do you live here alone?"

Anya paused for a moment as though considering the question. "Yes, I'm alone. You are also?"

Hazel nodded. Unless one wanted to count Mr. Kitty and his new friend, along with a moody ghost. "I've lived in town for a while but fell in love with this old house and recently purchased it."

Anya gazed past Hazel's shoulder in the direction of Clarabelle's house, though Hazel knew she couldn't see it for the mass of trees. "I believe it's several hundred years old."

She wished she could tell her that it had once belonged to her grandmother. "That's part of why I love it. It's obviously been upgraded from the original structure, but it still carries the feel of the past."

Anya shifted her stance. "The charm and the history are why I stay even though..."

The hint of mystery tugged hard on Hazel. As much as she knew she shouldn't press for unspoken information, she couldn't help herself. "Even though?" Hazel smiled to soften the question.

"Even though most don't like me here. But my muse loves the atmosphere, and I'm afraid if I leave, my paintings won't be the same."

Hazel wanted to continue down the path that followed the part about most didn't like her, but Anya was obviously trying to steer the conversation in a new direction. Hazel didn't want to ruin their friendship right off the bat by pressing too hard.

"You're a painter. Wow. That's amazing. What do you paint?"

Anya glanced around, looking high and low. "Different parts of this place. Flowers. Trees. Insects. They all inspire me."

Hazel nodded. "I can see how that would be true."

Anya tilted her head to the side as she regarded Hazel. "I have a painting of your house. Would you like to see?"

Interest sparked bright inside her. "Are you kidding? Of course."

Anya gave her the first real smile since they'd met. "My studio is around back."

Hazel followed her along the path constructed of large, flat pieces of stone. Tufts of grass grew between the cracks. Pink and red hollyhocks along the side swayed with the soft breeze.

"How ever did you manage to keep your flowers looking so great after all that heat?"

Anya glanced back over her shoulder. "Lots of water and luck, I guess."

Hazel had thought she'd given her petunias at the teashop lots of water, too, but they'd failed to thrive.

The stone pathway led to a smaller version of the cottage, but it had been styled the same. A small teakwood table with only one chair next to it sat near the door to the studio.

Anya opened the door and stepped inside. She waited for Hazel to follow before she closed it.

The scent of paint lingered in the air of the one-room studio. Gorgeous watercolors decorated nearly every inch of the walls. One with stately pine trees backed by an ominous sky hung next to a closeup of a bright pink rose with a fat bee hovering near its center.

"The painting of your house is over here," Anya said.

Hazel shifted her gaze to where Anya pointed and immediately fell in love. Anya had painted Clarabelle's house with evening sun streaming down in ethereal rivers from a bruised sky. The effect cast the white house with a pinkish glow that left Hazel feeling like the building was alive.

"This is incredible, Anya. There's so much energy and beauty. It's as though it's not an inanimate object, like it has a life of its own."

Anya's eyes lit with happiness. "That's the effect I was hoping for."

Hazel couldn't take her gaze off it. "It's so amazing. So perfect. I don't know that anyone could have captured the feel of the place any better."

She turned to her new friend. "You seem to have a knack for sensing what lies beneath and the ability to transfer that to your paintings."

Her cheeks pinkened. She smiled and looked away. "I don't know if I'd go that far, but I am able to live off what I make."

Hazel turned to another picture and immediately recognized it as the river where she and Peter loved to explore. She pointed to it. "This is right across the street, isn't it? I love that old bridge."

Anya nodded. "I love the energy there."

The mention of energy caught Hazel's attention. "Do you often sense energy from other people and things?"

Everything about her suddenly shut down, surprising Hazel. "If you're suggesting I'm a witch, I'm not."

Hazel held up her hands, palms facing Anya. "Oh, no. Of course not. I would never suggest that to anyone in this town even if I thought they might be. A hint of the word, witch, sends everyone into a frenzy."

Anya chuckled. "Like when they were throwing holy water balloons at everyone?"

She grinned. "Exactly."

Hazel studied her friend for a moment. "You seem to know a lot about what happens in Stonebridge, yet I never see you in town."

Anya turned to her workbench. She scooped up several paintbrushes and placed them in a metal can. "I do most of my shopping in Salem. Not that I get out that much anyway."

Hazel had a hard time believing others wouldn't like her. "Because of problems with some in town?"

She wadded used paper towels and tossed them in the trash. "Most people."

The need to know outmanned her manners this time. "Why do you think they don't like you?"

Sharp pain flashed in her eyes. "I don't think, Hazel. I know. They don't like me because they think I've ruined my husband."

But she'd said she lived there alone. "You're married?"

"Separated. Estranged. Whatever you want to call it."

Anya inhaled a deep breath and released it. "Eighteen months ago, we'd had a big fight, and I'd asked him to leave. I'd meant for him to go for the night until we'd cooled off, but Isaac walked out and never came back."

Hazel's intrigue kicked in full force. "What happened to him? Did he just disappear?"

"Oh, no. He's living somewhere outside Boston. I saw him once at his mother's house. He seems to be fine, but we haven't spoken since."

"People aren't going to dislike you because of that."

Desperation ruled her expression to the point she looked like she might cry. "He said some really horrible things about me around town. Things that weren't true."

"That doesn't mean everyone believed him."

She nodded. "He's an extrovert, so he's good friends with a lot of people in the area. I'm introverted, and others' emotions wear me down, so I tend to stick to myself. They know him better and, therefore, believed him."

Hazel frowned. There were so many good and intelligent people in this town. Why were they so easily led astray? "I'm sorry to hear that. It must make your life difficult."

Some of her emotion dissipated, and she shrugged. "If I keep to myself, I don't really have trouble. I prefer it that way anyway."

She supposed that made sense. "Well, I hope you don't mind if we become friends. I'll try not to take up too much of your emotional space." She followed with a warm smile.

Relief flooded from Anya and into Hazel. "I'd like that very much. You're a good soul, Hazel. A kind person. I sense that very strongly."

"You keep mentioning energy and sensing. You're very in tune with the vibes from others, aren't you?"

Wariness popped out first, but then Anya relaxed. "It's not something I'll admit often. They get all weird about it. But, yes. I seem to have this ability to read people and their moods."

"So, not a witch, but maybe a highly-sensitive person?"

Anya exhaled and smiled. "Exactly. That was part of the problem between Isaac and me. He'd lie about stuff, but I could tell what he thought, so I'd call him on it. In fact, the night he left, we'd fought about money that he'd said he needed for car repairs, but I could tell he was lying. He didn't like that very much."

Life could be hard. "It sounds like maybe you're better off without him."

She nodded. "Most definitely. I should probably file for divorce, but then I'd have to see him or engage with him again. I don't want to. I don't plan to marry again, so I've just let it be. I suppose at some point I'll have to address it."

Hazel tipped her head in agreement. "Hey, how would you like to come to my house tomorrow morning for tea? I could make omelets, too. Plus, I picked up an amazing cantaloupe at the farmer's market the other day."

Anya's eyes brightened. "Sounds wonderful. What can I bring?"

"Nothing. Just yourself is plenty enough."

"I'll be there. Does eight work?"

"Sounds great." Hazel gestured toward her house. "I'd better get back. My assistant opened the shop this morning, but she'll be expecting me soon. I'll see you tomorrow."

Hazel headed out with a smile on her face. She'd been worried what Anya had thought of her for no reason at all. Even if Anya did suspect her of being a witch, she wouldn't tell. She didn't really talk to anyone anyway.

* * *

The following morning, Hazel brewed a pot of Happy Day tea with a smile on her face. After meeting Anya, she'd looked forward to visiting with her more again that morning. Hazel had asked Gretta about Anya when she'd gone into the teashop the day before. Her assistant had agreed that she'd never gotten to know Anya, but she hadn't harbored any ill feelings toward her, either.

Maybe Anya only perceived that people didn't like her. Or maybe a select few believed her estranged husband, but that didn't account for the majority. She'd be sure to ask Peter when she saw him, too. As a police chief who kept his finger on the pulse of the community, as he liked to put it, he'd know more of the story.

With the tea happily brewing, Hazel moved to the cupboard and removed the teacups with violets hand-painted around the rim. The single violet inside on the bottom of the cup always made her smile. Something to look forward to seeing when she'd finished her tea.

Rapid thumping on her front door was a jolt to her peaceful morning.

Anya, if that's who was out there, repeated the pounding before Hazel reached the living room, sending her emotions into a frenzy. She quickened her pace to the front door and opened it.

Anya stood on the porch, her face eerily white like a morning mist coming off the ocean. Fear reflected bright in her eyes and radiated from her, hot and thick.

"Hazel." She panted. "Oh, God. Hazel. He's dead."

* * *

You can find IT'S ALL SIXES, Teas and Temptations Cozy Mystery Series, Book Six, on Amazon.com.

Book List

TEAS & TEMPTATIONS COZY MYSTERIES (PG-Rated Fun):
Once Wicked
Twice Hexed
Three Times Charmed
Four Warned
The Fifth Curse
It's All Sixes
Spellbound Seven
Elemental Eight
Nefarious Nine

BLACKWATER CANYON RANCH (Western Sexy Romance):
Caleb
Oliver
Justin
Piper
Jesse

ASPEN SERIES (Small Town Sexy Romance):
Wounded (Prequel)
Relentless
Lawless
Cowboys and Angels
Come Back to Me
Surrender
Reckless
Tempted
Crazy One More Time

I'm With You
Breathless

PINECONE VALLEY (Small Town Sexy Romance):
Love Me Again
Love Me Always

RETRIBUTION NOVELS (Sexy Romantic Suspense):
Branded
Hunted
Banished
Hijacked
Betrayed

ARGENT SPRINGS (Small Town Sexy Romance):
Whispers
Secrets

OTHER TITLES:
Moonlight and Margaritas (Sexy Contemporary Romance)
Sweet Vengeance (Sexy Romantic Suspense)

About the Author

Award-winning author Cindy Stark lives with her family and a sweet Border Collie in a small town shadowed by the Rocky Mountains. She writes fun, witch cozy mysteries, emotional romantic suspense, and sexy contemporary romance. She loves to hear from readers!

Connect with her online at:
http://www.CindyStark.com
http://facebook.com/CindyStark19
https://www.amazon.com/Cindy-Stark/e/B008FT394W

Printed in Great Britain
by Amazon

69350392R00099